Animal Kingdom

by Iain Rob Wright

SalGad Publishing Group
Worcestershire, UK

SalGad Publishing Group
Redditch, Worcestershire/UK
www.iainrobwright.com

Publisher's Note: This is a work of fiction. Names, characters, places, and incidents are a product of the author's imagination. Locales and public names are sometimes used for atmospheric purposes. Any resemblance to actual people, living or dead, or to businesses, companies, events, institutions, or locales is completely coincidental.

Book Layout & Design ©2015 - BookDesignTemplates.com

Ordering Information:
Quantity sales. Special discounts are available on quantity purchases by corporations, associations, and others. For details, contact the "Special Sales Department" at the address above.

Animal Kingdom/ Iain Rob Wright. -- 2nd ed.
ISBN 978-1492986379

BOOKS BY IAIN ROB WRIGHT

Animal Kingdom
2389
Holes in the Ground (with J.A.Konrath)
Sam
ASBO
The Final Winter
The Housemates
Sea Sick
Ravage
Savage
The Picture Frame
Wings of Sorrow
The Gates
Tar
Soft Target
Hot Zone
End Play

For our loyalist friends, the pets.

""We can always be human
Meeting each day a wise new man
But the Animal Kingdom to which we belong
Animals we are; this truth can't be wrong." "

–**Munia Khan**, *Beyond the Venal Mind*

CHAPTER 1

JOE TUGGED HIS jacket closed as the chilled autumn air sought out the unguarded crevices of his body. The gloomy sky drizzled down to earth and coated everything in dullness, to a point where it seemed that colour no longer existed in the world. But the dreary weather was not enough to dampen Joe's spirits. Today was a good day. He was spending the day with his son.

Exuberant Danny lingered nearby, peering through the bars of the zoo's famous Silverback exhibit. Disappointingly, the leafy enclosure was currently vacant of its illustrious inhabitant. Joe knew that his son would be upset by the animal's absence but, as was the case with eight-year old boys, his attention span soon reset itself and it wasn't long before he was running off in a new direction entirely.

"Dad! That man over there is being attacked by a snake."

Joe stared down at his son, amazed, as always, that his watery-blue eyes could look so much like his own. "Don't be silly, Danny," he said, breath turning to steam in the cold air. "That's just the zoo's snake handler. He's about to do a show."

"I want to go see!" Danny tugged at his father's arm, deceptively strong for such a slender child wearing a Bret 'The Hitman' Hart t-shirt and Velcro trainers. "Hurry, before we miss anything."

Joe allowed himself to be dragged toward a three-sided lean-to shelter erected besides the zoo's moss-covered WORLD OF VENOM building. It had been designed to look as if it were made of bamboo reeds, but the façade was unconvincing.

A uniformed man entered the structure from a rear access and be-gan positioning plastic crates on a wooden table. Each of the containers held various species of reptiles, insects, and spiders. The man's tanned-leather skin matched his khaki clothing and was weathered, brown and loose. He had a boa constrictor the length of a scaffold pole wrapped around his bony shoulders, but seemed completely at ease with it.

Danny jumped up and down excitedly. "Sweet! I bet that thing could squish him to death real easy!"

"Don't be so morbid, Danny!"

"Sorry, Dad. I just think it's cool."

"It's okay. I just want you to think nice things. Come on, let's get closer." Joe took Danny's hand – half the size of his own – and pushed through the gathering crowd of adults and their children. It wasn't difficult to get to the front of a group when you were as freakishly tall as Joe. People tended to get out of his way long before he had to ask them.

"Look at the size of that thing, Dad!" At the front of the growing audience – now close to a dozen people – Danny started jumping up and down again, his wispy blond hair flopping around in the musty breeze. Childish glee oozed off him in ribbons.

The snake handler turned his attention to them both. Joe cringed, waiting to get a reprimand for his son's nuisance behaviour. Fortunately, however, the uniformed man just smiled at them instead.

"Hey there, young un," the handler said to Danny. "You like snakes?"

"Yeah, I do. Jake the Snake used to have one called Damien."

The snake handler wrinkled his forehead, readjusted the slithering reptile in his arms, and then said, "Isn't that a wrestler from years back?"

Danny nodded enthusiastically. "My dad has lots of old tapes and I watch 'em every weekend when I stay over. My bestest favourite is The Undertaker. Check it out!" He spun around to show the man the design on his backpack.

"Undertaker rip?" said the handler, confused.

Danny spun back around and giggled. "No, silly! Rest in peace. It's what The Undertaker says to everyone right before he beats them up with his tombstone." He rolled his eyes back into his head so that only the whites were showing, and then repeated the words in his best attempt at a gravelly, adult voice. "Rest...In...Peeeaaaace."

The crowd laughed, so did the snake handler, struggling with his giant brown reptile between each chuckle. He pulled the animal down, away from his face, and then smiled over at Joe. "Fine little lad you have there, sir."

"Thanks. He's a handful though. Just like your snake."

"You can say that again! She's really unsettled today. Won't keep still for a minute, bless her."

"Sounds just like my son."

Danny bopped him on the arm. "Hey! I'm nothing like a snake. I'm gunna tell Mum on you."

The crowd laughed again, this time giving a collective "Oooooooo!"

Joe knew his son was just showing off, but it was nice to see him come out of his shell. After the last few years, with the divorce and everything else, it was good to see that Danny had any confidence left at all.

Joe rustled Danny's hair, messing it up more than it already was. "We best be moving on, little dude," he said, "or we won't fit everything in. Say goodbye to the nice man and his snake."

Danny twisted his face into a frown, but did as he was told. His shoulders slumped as he spoke. "See ya, Mister. Thanks for letting... Hey Mister...are you okay?"

Joe was alerted by the tone of his son's voice before he actually saw anything was wrong. Even when he saw the problem, he wasn't sure whether or not to be concerned.

The snake handler was struggling with the huge reptile around his shoulders. The animal had coiled its way around his ribcage and was tightening.

"Step away, Danny." Joe moved in front of his son, keeping him back from the wooden barrier that separated the crowd from the lean-to shelter. The slithering reptile had begun to form a noose around the keeper's neck and was slowly constricting with each convulsion of its muscular body. The crowd started to murmur, the first gentle stages of panic taking hold.

No one knows if this is just part of the act.

But it can't be. This man is really struggling.

The snake handler began to choke and threw out his arms out in desperation. Joe jumped the barrier and dashed toward the shelter just as the struggling man dropped to his knees on the plank-wood flooring. The fragile walls of the bamboo shelter shook beneath the impact.

"Stay calm," Joe shouted in a voice that was the exact opposite. He reached out to grab the snake, but recoiled immediately.

Whoa! Do I really wanna put my hands on this thing? Can it bite me?

Joe allowed himself to hesitate only a moment longer then gave himself a mental shove. Come on! There's a man's life at stake. Do something!

He snatched at the thick reptile, fighting away revulsion as his fingers made contact with the rough, quivering flesh that was cold to the touch. Several seconds of frantic tugging made no difference at all. The snake's grip became even tighter. The desperate handler turned a deep purple as the pressure pushed his eyeballs a half-inch out of their sockets, making them bulge. Joe felt a wave of sickness crash through his insides.

I can't do anything. I can't get this thing off of him. I never watched a man die before...

Joe turned to the anxious crowd and checked that his son was nearby. "Don't just stand there!" he shouted at the group of startled strangers. "Somebody go get help! Danny, you stay where you are and close your eyes, okay? Everything is fine." He could tell by his son's fearful expression that he didn't believe that things were 'fine'.

Moving back around, Joe saw that blood trickled from both of the snake handler's nostrils. The slithering beast, clamped around the man's throat, glared at Joe, malevolent eyes boring into his flesh. Its forked-tongue flicked back and forth, tasting the air.

People in the crowd started backing away as if they somehow thought the snake handler's peril was infectious. Some of them scattered immediately, crying out for help as they fled in all directions, while others backed away in silence, unable to take their eyes off the harrowing scene in front of them. Joe didn't retreat with either group. He was rooted to the spot.

Locked in a death stare with a nine-foot Boa Constrictor.

"Dad!"

The sound of Danny's voice allowed Joe to regain control of his senses, like being dragged out of water by an unseen hand. He spun around to find that his son had approached the wooden barrier and was about to crouch underneath it.

Joe flung out an arm and shouted. "Stay there, Danny! I'll handle th-"

From the corner of his eye, Joe sensed movement. He turned just in time to see the snake strike. The adrenaline in his body pumped his reactions just enough that he was able to lunge aside, a mere split-second before the murderous reptile sliced its fangs through the air. The snake handler flopped face down on the boards. The boa constrictor slithered out from beneath his body. The man was dead.

Holy cow!

"Dad, I'm scared!"

Joe sprang into action, exiting the shelter and vaulting the barrier. He scooped Danny up in his arms and chased after the fleeing crowd. Help still had not arrived, but it hardly mattered anymore now that the snake handler was dead.

Someone still needs to grab that snake though.

And then destroy the effing thing!

Joe kept his lanky strides fast, yet steady, not wanting to trip and fall on the unforgiving pavement whilst carrying his son. Blood pounded in his eardrums. All around him people scattered in different directions. It was strange to see just how many people were panicking. There had been perhaps a dozen men and women at the snake handler's hut – along with a handful of children – but as Joe looked around now, he saw at least five times that many.

Why are so many people in a hurry to get their asses out of here? What else is happening?

Joe slowed down and eventually stopped, turning to look back where he'd come from. The huge boa constrictor was still inside the lean-to shelter, slithering over the lifeless body of its ex-handler. It was reason enough to panic, for sure, but Joe was certain that only those nearby would have noticed the tragedy. Something else must have been scaring people.

Another animal attack? Impossible.

Joe glanced around the zoo, examining the multiple animal enclosures and exhibit buildings that lined the grass-edged pathways. A racket was coming from each of them, as if the caged specimens inside were agitated by something. The hoots and howls from the monkey compounds were particularly loud and Joe could see the various primates rattling their bars with reckless fury. Joe could feel the vibrations from the steel bars in his teeth.

What is happening?

He decided he didn't want to wait and find out. He needed to make sure his son was safe – from what exactly, he did not know. Danny was rigid in his arms, making no sound other than the wet panting of his breath.

"Everything's going to be okay, buddy," he said soothingly. "Let me get you someplace quiet and we can sit down and have a Coke."

Joe started moving again, a sense of urgency seizing his internal organs and pumping them like pistons. Some deep-buried instinct told him he needed to get away from the area as quickly as possible. Up ahead was the zoo's brand-new visitor centre, B.R. ZOOLOGICAL INSTITUTE AND ENVIROMENTAL CENTRE. The lengthy glass structure's recent grand opening was advertised all over the park and it looked like as good a place as any to find some authority.

Joe picked up speed, his worn trainers wearing thinner against the harsh grey cement of the pathways. All around him people were still panicking, scuttling in all directions like frenzied ants. It was still unclear what was causing all of the chaos, but Joe knew it was more than just a snake attack. Something else was happening.

Something bad.

The visitor's centre seemed to grow in size as Joe got closer to it. He could make out the large glass doors of its entrance. Several people had already begun to move inside, but a vast majority were running right past the building – likely heading towards the car park beyond. Joe wondered whether their idea was a good one.

I just want to get indoors. I don't know what's going on yet, but I know that a load of people panicking in their cars is gonna have a bad ending.

Joe broke off from the crowd and approached the visitor centre, hopping up a set of brick steps that joined with a decorative patio at the front of the building. A middle-aged Black man with grey sideburns was standing amongst the potted trees and plants. He quickly moved aside when he saw he was in Joe's way. Joe nodded a 'thanks' to the man before moving through the building's wide-open double-doors.

The fluorescent lights inside were dazzling after the bleak grey of outside. The first thing Joe's eyes managed to focus on was a large rectangular sign hanging from the ceiling. It declared the room to be THE EDUCATION HALL.

The area was full of life-like exhibits: African elephants, alligators, rhinos, and many other imposing creatures – each of the models stared at the centre of the room with their soulless glass eyes. Several other people stood inside with Joe. Each of them looked as concerned and freaked out as he was. There was only a single zoo employee amongst them all, given away by his bright-green waist-jacket against a khaki-coloured uniform. He wore the tatty, round spectacles of an intellectual man and his neatly-combed grey hair only added to that impression. He looked as dumfounded as everybody else. Joe still considered him the best person to speak to.

Nearby, several plush, cube-shaped chairs of varying colours were arranged in front of a vast LCD screen showing nature documentaries. Joe eased Danny down onto a purple cube and gave him a quick hug. "Just wait here one sec, buddy, okay?"

Danny nodded and sat still.

Joe examined his son for a few moments, saw how frightened he was, and then kissed his forehead. "I'm proud of you, son."

The zoo employee had moved over to the far wall of the hall and was fiddling with a canary-yellow rubber-cased walkie-talkie. It didn't seem like the man was having much success in gaining information if his wrinkled, frustrated brow was anything to go by. Joe approached the man slowly, trying to seem calm rather than agitated. It like rationality could be at a premium right now.

The zoo keeper looked up at Joe. "Sir, may I help you?"

"Hello," Joe replied. "Do you know what the heck is going on?"

The man shook his head and his spectacles jittered on the bridge of his narrow nose. He readjusted them before speaking. "Not the foggiest, I'm afraid, and I can't reach any of the zoo keepers to find out. A couple of the visitors I've spoken to have mentioned animal attacks, but they were too distressed to provide details. Seems very unlikely."

Joe thought about the snake attack. "You don't think an animal attack is possible?"

"Possible? Yes. But extremely unlikely. The enclosures are secure and the staff are extremely dedicated, experienced professionals. There's never been an incident of such a kind in the seven years I've worked here."

"Sorry to disagree," Joe said, "but I just watched a large snake kill one of your staff about ten minutes ago, over by the World of Venom building – a boa constrictor, I think. It squeezed the poor guy to death in front of a dozen people."

The employee's face dropped. "Terry? I pray that you are mistaken, sir, I truly do. Terry has been with us for many years and loved Betsy a great deal."

Joe raised an eyebrow. "Betsy?"

"Yes, Betsy. She is the zoo's Pearl Island Boa. She's always been extremely gentle. I can't believe she would ever attack anyone – least of all Terry. They had a...bond, for want of a better word."

Joe nodded. He didn't want to upset the man further, until he understood what was happening. "Maybe he's okay," Joe supposed. "It did all happen very suddenly."

The other man thought about things for a moment and his expression seemed to get grimmer with each passing second. Finally, he looked back up at Joe and said, "I believe you, sir. It doesn't seem like you're lying and I see no reason why you would. Something is obviously going on here today, but I just cannot fathom the idea that any of our animals would attack their handlers. There are too many precautions."

"Look, I don't mean to be impatient, but you're the only representative of the zoo I could find. You need to do something."

"And what exactly would you have me do? I am a curator, not a crowd controller."

Joe sighed. "Nevertheless, you have a responsibility."

The man looked at Joe for several seconds before sagging at the shoulders and replying. "I suppose you're right. I should find out what's going on." He pushed Joe aside, headed for the front of the hall, and spoke over his shoulder as he went. "I still don't believe things are as bad as people are–"

Joe turned around to see why the curator had stopped mid-sentence. He could hardly believe his eyes as people started to scream in terror.

Four lions blocked the far entrance to the visitor's centre and were snarling at the people inside. Each of their fangs was the size of a tent peg and freshly spilled blood dripped from their jaws.

Joe had a feeling that he was about to have a very bad day.

CHAPTER 2

JOE DIDN'T KNOW why he needed to state the obvious, but saying it out loud was the only way he could accept what was happening. "Those are goddamn Lions!"

The curator hurried back toward Joe. "This is not possible," he said, his voice trembling like lime-jelly. "The enclosures are too secure for dangerous animals to get loose."

Joe grabbed the man's collar and shook him. "Think about how they got loose later, okay! I need to get my son somewhere safe, right now."

The curator seemed to accept the situation and nodded his head quickly. "We should...we should get everyone further inside the building. It will be safer there."

Without further comment, Joe raced over to get Danny from the cube seats. The boy was frozen solid, eyes fixed on the slinking predators entering the hall. Joe took his son into his arms and turned back towards the zoo's curator. "Where can we g--"

The sound of fresh screams cut Joe off. Four lions, led by a heavily-maned male, were now fully inside the building. Two females split off to corner a young brunette woman in the gap between two snack machines. The beasts toyed with her, swatting her back and forth. Blood formed on the woman's white blouse where a set of razor-sharp claws succeeded in penetrating her flesh. Elsewhere, the remaining two lions pursued anyone unable to find a hiding space.

"We have to help these people," Joe said. "Take my son somewhere safe."

The curator quickly took Danny into his arms, then turned to Joe. "We'll be in the research wing, through the red door in the far corner. I suggest you come with us now not later."

Joe nodded, "I'll be right behind you." Then he ran off towards the brunette woman between the snack machines. He came to a sudden stop when he encountered the male lion ripping out the throat of an elderly gentleman. The big cat's jaws cut off the old man's screams and left him gargling blood. Joe swallowed back the burger and fries he'd eaten that morning, and battled with the dizziness that erupted from the base of his stomach.

How did this happen? People aren't supposed to get eaten alive by lions in the middle of England. This isn't Jumanji!

More screaming. People being ripped to shreds. Torn apart. Somehow the young brunette was still managing to fend off the two lionesses, kicking out at them each time they attacked and swatting at them with her handbag. It was working – for now – but it wouldn't be long before her timing was slightly off and the lions got a grip on her.

Joe grabbed one of the coloured cube-seats and hoisted it up to his chest. It was heavy – very heavy. Joe sucked in a deep breath and heaved with all his might, just about managing to get the thing up above his head. Then, like a circus strongman, he waddled across the hall towards the two attacking lionesses. The male lion also nearby, ripping apart another victim: this time a young girl.

I must be insane. The first weekend I've had with Danny in a month and it ends up with me taking on a pride of lions with a chair from IKEA.

Without allowing himself to think anymore – or back out altogether – Joe flung the cube as hard as he could. Through some stroke of fortune the heavy piece of furniture barrelled into both of the lionesses at the snack machines, hitting them like a bowling ball striking a pair of skittles. The lionesses sprawled onto their sides, their attack on the young woman ceasing temporarily.

"Come on!" Joe shouted, holding out his hand.

The woman looked at him, quaking with fear against one of the snack machines. The shock in her round, hazel-brown eyes made her seem more like a cartoon character than a human being.

"Come on!" Joe shouted at her again, louder.

Finally, the woman started to move, edging toward him slowly.

Get yourself moving, woman! I don't fancy dying today.

One lioness was back on her feet, coiled up, ready to pounce. The young woman saw this and froze. She looked at Joe pleadingly.

There was only one thing on Joe's mind and he expressed it earnestly. "RUN!"

Thankfully, the woman did as directed. The two of them bolted. Up ahead, people screamed hysterically, rational thought blocked by sheer terror and incomprehension. Joe wanted to help them all. He shouted as loudly as he could while still running. "Get in the next room. Everyone, follow me!"

Joe's words were almost pointless. One or two people responded, racing after him towards safety, but a majority of the people continued to stand and scream aimlessly. There was nothing Joe could do for these people. They couldn't even help themselves.

Up ahead on the left was a red-painted door reading: STAFF ONLY. Joe was sure it led to what the curator had called "The Research Wing."

Roaring – from behind Joe – so loud it made his fillings ache. Without looking, he knew that the lions were giving chase, their instincts unable to resist the sight of fleeing prey. He could almost feel their rancid, blood-soaked breath on the back of his neck. He expected to feel their wicked claws slicing through the sinewy fibres of his hamstrings any second. Joe picked up as much speed as he could muster.

He just prayed it was enough.

Enough to outrun a lion...

When he and a handful of others reached the red door, Joe slammed right into it, unable to slow down in time to stop. It was then that he noticed the entrance was locked, an ominous steel number pad set beside it on the wall. He bashed at it with his fists, hammering until his skin cracked, but it would not swing open. Behind Joe, the other strangers gathered frantically. Behind them, all four lions approached, led by the male with the thick, blood-soaked mane.

"What do we do?" asked the young brunette woman.

Joe shook his head. "I don't know."

To his surprise, she laughed. "Fabulous!"

The lions were upon them fast. The assembled group shoved one another, battling to get to the back where it was safer. Those at the front began screaming. One man, dressed in a grubby chef's uniform, was knocked forwards onto his knees by the people behind.

The lions were on him in seconds.

As a single unit, the muscled predators pounced, pinning the chef to the floor with their huge round paws. The male lion was the first to draw blood, tearing off a chunk of stringy flesh from the chef's neck with its powerful jaws. A torrent of steaming blood arced high into the air and spattered his grubby white tunic.

At least Danny will be safe, Joe thought to himself through the growing haze of his fear-soaked mind. Even if his father gets eaten by a lion. Little bit of therapy and he'll be fine.

Joe swallowed hard.

He watched the ensuing chaos and finally lost all feeling – from each of his fingertips to all ten of his toes. He could no longer think in a straight line, the adrenaline dissipating through his body and sending him into a dazed void of inaction. One-by-one, the members of the group were taken down by the lions, bitten and mauled like ragdolls. It would not be long until Joe's turn was next; the three or four people in front of him were his only protection.

He met the glare of the male lion's amber-flecked eyes.

A rumbling growl erupted from the animal's gore-encrusted mouth.

Can't believe this is how I'm going to die. A footnote in 'Ripley's Believe it or not.'

The people in front of Joe fell quickly, kicking out and fighting with every ounce of spirit they had left, but dying anyway. It was inevitable.

Joe stood motionless, unable to help anyone or himself – a helpless voyeur of the human tragedy going on all around him.

One by one, people screamed and then died.

Eventually, Joe's turn to join them arrived.

The male lion glared at him once again.

Then all four lions snarled. All four lions pounced.

Joe closed his eyes.

Unseen hands grabbed him, pulling him backwards. He fell hard onto his side, the impact stealing his breath away. It was a full moment later, when the vision-stars cleared, that he found himself lying in a cramped corridor. Other people were piling in after him, pushing and heaving through the narrow gap of the doorway. There were further screams from those unlucky enough not to make it through.

A hand grabbed Joe around the shoulder. When he looked up, he saw that it belonged to the grey-haired curator. Joe got to his feet with difficulty, still struggling for breath. "Where's...my...son?"

"Over there." The curator pointed to a bench against the wall. Danny sat there, safe and sound, yet clearly terrified. Joe's lungs deflated as the stress and terror finally fled the rigid fibres of his body. His son was unharmed. He could relax.

"We have to get that door locked back up," the curator asserted. "I'm sorry I didn't realise it had locked behind me. Those poor people."

"Forget about it," Joe snapped. "There're still people still out there now. We have to help them."

"We cannot. You've already helped as many as you can, and if we don't get that door secured, then none of us will be safe."

Joe knew the logic was correct, but it didn't make the decision any easier. He thought about Danny's safety and made up his mind. "Okay. Let's get that door closed."

Joe and the curator rushed over to the thick wooden door and pushed against it, shoving back the half-score of desperate people clambering at the other side. There were agonised pleas and prayers to God – desperate begging that the door not be closed – but there was no hope to save them all – or any of them. In fact, most of the people outside were already half-torn, limb hanging from limb. Even those still mobile were bleeding and shocked, wandering around like shell-shocked teenagers on the beaches of Omaha.

Except for one man further back who was still managing to put up a fight.

It was the guy from earlier, Joe noticed. The guy from the patio.

The Black man with the grey sideburns had shown politeness to Joe earlier. Now the man was desperately fighting off the lions and trying to help others under attack. He wielded a fire extinguisher and was spraying foam into the faces of the lions, forcing them to back away, disorientated.

"He's trying to save everyone," said Joe, and for a moment he thought the man might just do it.

But then the male lion took him down, blindsiding the courageous man as he concentrated his blinding fog on one of the lionesses. Joe heard the man cry out as he hit the deck hard. If it wasn't for the extinguisher in his hands, blocking the lethal bite of the lion, the guy would already be dead.

Joe glanced around, noticed that the three lionesses were still disorientated, pawing at their faces as they tried to clear the foam from their airways.

Just the male left. I can help this guy.

Joe stopped thinking. He forced his rubbery legs to take form and he exited the safety of the corridor and went back into the Education Hall. Exertion made his knees feel like hot coals inside paper sacks.

The struggling man was still unharmed, fending off several attacks by using the metal fire extinguisher as a shield.

Joe picked up his pace.

Reaching the male lion, he swung his leg into the hardest kick he could muster. His foot connected with the side of the lion's head and a sharp, white-hot jolt of electric pain shot through his toes. The blow had almost no effect on the target, however. The male lion flinched from the attack, but seemed no more than merely irritated.

Bugger it!

The lion let out an almighty roar. It was at this point that the Black man readjusted the fire extinguisher's nozzle and pulled back the handle. Gloopy jets of foam shot into the male lion's mouth, cutting off its ear-splitting roar and reducing it to a startled whimper. The big cat leapt backwards, choking, hacking, and rubbing its maw along the floor.

Joe pulled the other man up and the two of them galloped back towards the red doorway as quickly as their battered bodies would allow them. All around, fierce lions lay mewling like wounded kittens. The whole effed-up situation was surreal – like Alice in Wonderland on crack.

The two men passed through the door into the corridor. The waiting curator slammed it shut immediately behind them. The automatic bolt let out an echoing clack!

Joe slumped back against the door and took a steady breath. It seemed like the first in a long time and the air stabbed his lungs as if he were breathing in carpet tacks. His heart was threatening to rip right through his chest. But at least Danny was still safe, still sitting on the bench against wall. The young brunette woman sat beside him, apparently making conversation and trying to calm his nerves – or perhaps her own. Joe's heartbeat slowed down a little, but he couldn't help shake the feeling that things were not yet over.

In fact, he had a feeling they were going to get worse.

CHAPTER 3

"TIME I LEARNED your name, sir."

"It's Joe."

The curator shook his hand. "My name is Mason. I am the head curator of the zoo and I thank you for all your help. I don't think I could have taken charge like you did."

"Just wish so many people hadn't gotten hurt. How many made it?"

"There's seven of us, including you and you son, but even more people would have been injured if it wasn't for you, Joe. You're a hero and people owe you their li-"

A short, pudgy man with neatly-combed oil-black hair wedged himself between the two of them. He glared up at Mason. "Perhaps you two could stop flirting for one moment and tell me what the hell is going on! I can tell you right now that this wretched place will never open its doors to the public again after I'm through with it."

Mason's expression did not change. "And who might you be, sir?"

The pudgy man's features scrunched up in disapproval. "Who am I? Who am I? I am Christopher-bloody-Randall! That's who I am."

Mason shook his head. "I'm sorry?"

"From Black Remedy Investments plc. You know, the company that paid for this very building you're standing in right now? Show me a little more respect, because I have a good mind to demand our investment back right now. This is not what I expected when I came here for a simple business meeting this morning. It's a fiasco."

Again, without any discernible expression, Mason shook his head. "I'm afraid I don't involve myself with the zoo's finances. That would be the concern of the park administrators. I apologise for any inconvenience to you, Mr Randall, but I think you can clearly see that we are all equally affected by the day's events."

The angry little man went bright red now and began to wheeze. Spittle formed at the corners of his bulbous lips. "Now you listen here. I own this building, which means I own you. I need to get out of here immediately, do you hear me? My business here is finished and I have a very important meeting to get--"

Joe had heard enough. "Look, mate, I don't know what mental illness you're currently taking medication for, but people are dead. Nobody gives two shits if you have a business meeting with the Queen. Unless you intend to be helpful, please just do us all a favour and fuck off! Excuse my French."

The investor spun to face Joe, toe to toe, but seemed to lose his spirit when he realised the difference in size and height. Joe probably weighed six-stone more than the man and towered over him like a lead statue.

The man still hadn't lost his attitude completely, though. "How dare you speak to me like that. Do you know who I am?"

"You're Lord Randall of Asshole-land. Thanks, got it, don't care. Just sit down while Mason and I actually try to do something constructive."

Randall shook with anger, glaring at Joe as if he were excrement on his Ralph Lauren loafers. Fortunately it seemed he had finally run out of patience and he stormed off down the corridor. Joe took the opportunity to glance over at Danny, wondering if he should go and check on him. His son had lain himself down across the brunette woman's lap and was nearly asleep. Joe decided to leave him alone for a few minutes more.

He turned his focus back to Mason. "That guy was a jackass."

Mason nodded. "Investors always are. Black Remedy bought shares in the zoo last year and they've acted like they own the place ever since. They don't see the zoo as way of preserving the world's great nature, they just see pound signs. Still, he has a right to be angry after what has happened today. No doubt he is correct about the zoo's future being rather bleak."

"How could this happen, Mason?"

"I really can't say. Nothing like this has ever happened before. All of the dangerous animals are kept inside high-security enclosures. The only way in or out is through twin-layer fences. You enter one, close it, and then open the second. There's no way an animal can escape."

Joe nodded. "I understand the type of thing you mean, but, whether it's plausible or not, the lions got out somehow."

"Indeed they did."

Joe waited for further comment, but it appeared that the curator had none to make, so he decided to speak instead. "Okay, just keep trying to reach someone on your radio. I'm going to go check on my son."

Mason nodded and Joe left him alone under the bright lights of the corridor. Over on the bench, Danny was still lying on the brunette woman's lap. She was stroking his head tenderly. Beneath the harsh light, Joe could see that the woman's wounds were shallow and already healing. She'd been lucky.

"Hey," Joe said as he approached her. "Thanks for looking after my son."

She smiled glumly and it was then that Joe saw she was in fact just a girl, not a woman. Dark bags beneath each of her eyes gave the impression that she was older, but her smooth white skin betrayed her real youth.

About twenty maybe?

"Least I can do after you saved my life," she said.

Joe blushed. "Wouldn't go that far."

"I would." The girl offered out her hand. It was slender and recently manicured, but many of the painted-pink nails were chipped and broken, probably from her ordeal between the snack machines. "I'm Grace."

Joe noticed a recently-healed scar that lined the back of her wrist, along with several older, faded wounds. He didn't want to be rude by staring, so he averted his eyes. "Pleased to meet you, Grace," he said and the two shook hands. "I'm Joe and this is--"

"Danny. Yeah, I know. He told me before taking a nap. He was worried about you out there. You shouldn't be such a hero."

Joe acknowledged his selfishness. If he'd been hurt then Danny would be all alone in this dangerous situation. What the hell was he thinking, running around out there like Joe-the-lion-tamer? He couldn't risk leaving Danny alone again.

I won't.

"Mind if I wake him?" he asked.

Grace laughed. The sound was delicate and fragile. "He's your son. Be my guest."

Joe knelt beside Danny and gently shook one of his tiny legs. "Hey, little dude! You awake?"

Danny opened his eyes slowly, pupils widening gradually like ink stains on cloth.

"Everything is okay now," said Joe. "Daddy's back."

Danny smiled and closed his eyes again as if wanting to get back to some wonderful dream. He muttered under his breath, "Can I stay here with Grace?"

Joe raised an eyebrow. It wasn't like Danny to form bonds so quickly – not since the divorce – but he supposed it couldn't hurt. Joe looked up at Grace. "That okay?"

Grace nodded. "Sure. Could kind of do with a rest myself. Wish I could just switch off like him."

"There's a quiet-room on the right," said Mason, approaching from down the corridor with walkie talkie still in hand. "It's where we put visitors when they're not feeling well. There's a sofa-bed inside."

"Excellent!" said Grace, her face lighting up like a beacon. "Come on, Danny."

Joe watched the girl lead his son to the room on the opposite side of the corridor before disappearing inside. For some reason he trusted her, and he relaxed knowing that Danny was in her care. Maybe it was the feeling of having a women's support that made him feel that way.

It's been a while.

Mason placed a hand on Joe's shoulder. "I couldn't reach anyone. I got some static and some garbled voices, but nothing I could get a fix on. From the brief connections I made, things seemed pretty bad. No one is answering."

Joe raised his eyebrows. "No one at all?"

Mason's stiff expression gave nothing away about his feelings, but Joe had a feeling the man was beginning to crack. Slender creases at the corners of his eyes seemed to widen as he spoke. "There are a dozen zoo keepers here today and they all carry walkie talkies – just like this one. Not one of them is replying. I can't imagine what that means."

"I can," said Joe, "and it's not a nice thing to think about. You tried phoning anyone outside the zoo?"

Mason shook his head. "That was what I was going to do next. There are phones in the offices upstairs. I should be able to call right through to the administration building at the rear entrance. Office staff don't generally work the weekends, but there's usually one or two people there on a Saturday. Mr Randall said he was here this morning for a meeting, so perhaps the members of the board are around too. They may be able to shed some light on the current situation."

"Good," said Joe, scratching the stubble on his wide chin. It seemed to have grown inches in just the last hour. "What about the building we're in? Can we get out any other way than the door we came through?"

"There's a fire exit at the end of this corridor and we can also enter the cafeteria, which has several more exits. I don't know if it would be wise to try to leave, however."

Joe looked up and down the corridor, taking in the scene of shellshocked survivors. In addition to the rude investor, Mr Randall, there was also an elderly woman with grey hair sitting right next to a heavily-tattooed bald man. It was a strange sight to see such opposites placed side-by-side.

"I think I agree," Joe said after some consideration. "My son and I are going nowhere until those lions are dealt with."

Mason adjusted his spectacles. "We should get everyone assembled and come up with a plan, even if it's only to sit and wait for rescue."

"Agreed," said Joe. "Is there somewhere more comfortable we can all go? I don't think people will be able to calm down in this corridor. It's too close to what happened."

Mason took Joe's arms and led him a few feet down the corridor. "There's a staffroom in this part of the building. It's a large area with enough places to sit and a few refreshments. I'd say it would be best place to reconvene for now. We can always move upstairs later if we need to. The building is pretty much empty, today being the weekend. They'll be plenty of room. In fact, I think we're the only ones here."

"Let's get going then."

Mason clapped his hands together and got the attention of the other shell-shocked survivors. "Okay everyone, can I have your attention, please?"

Silence from everyone. Glazed expressions and teary cheeks. From the other side of the exit door, the wet smacking sounds of lions feeding on corpses could be heard in vivid detail.

Mason continued, despite the lack of audience response. "We are going to follow this corridor down to its end and enter a staffroom beyond. It is comfortable there, warm and safe. We should gather whilst we wait to learn more about this...situation."

"And what is the situation?" asked the Black man with the grey sideburns. He was still carrying his dented fire extinguisher.

"We don't know," Mason answered. "Obviously there has been a breach in the lion enclosure, but as to how that happened, I do not know. I will try to contact the administration building shortly – and the emergency services of course – but first we need to get ourselves situated."

"Who are you to give orders?" It was the investor, Randall. The man's mood had obviously not improved.

"I am no one to give orders," Mason calmly told him, "but as the only one offering practical advice, I see no harm in having people do as I say for the time being."

"If you hadn't allowed this to happen in the first place then I would have a little more trust to afford to you, my friend."

"Mr Randall, if you feel better blaming me personally I am happy for you to do so, but my advice is that we group together somewhere more comfortable. If you or anybody else does not wish to follow that advice then you are free to do as you like. Those who do wish to follow my suggestion may come with myself and Joe, who, may I remind you, was the one that helped a majority of you in the first place."

"If that's your advice," said the man with grey sideburns. "Then that's what I'll do. I don't see the point in all this negativity and arguing." The last comment was directed at Randall who seemed less than impressed at being called out.

"Let's go then," said Joe. "I'll get Grace and my son and we'll be off in five."

A heavy thud rattled the red door behind them on its hinges. The lions were trying to break through into the corridor.

Joe's eyes widened. "Or maybe we should get going right now.

CHAPTER 4

RANDALL COULD NOT believe he was running down a corridor to get away from lions. It was the biggest screw-up he had ever known, and when it was all over this dump of a zoo would pay for it. To think his company had actually provided obscene amounts of cash to improve the facilities here. Positive publicity, the marketers had claimed. What a load of rubbish. He'd be claiming back every penny now and more. The place could rot for all he cared.

"This is ridiculous," said Randall – wheezing heavily – to a tattooed man running alongside him. "Don't they have guns here...or... or something in place to control animals when they...get loose?"

"Tell me about it!" The man's reply was in a thick Scottish accent. The word 'about' sounded like 'a-boot' from the man's uncouth mouth. "They must be running the place with a bunch of wee ten-year-olds. Someone is gonna be knee-deep in bother when this is over, mark my words."

Randall sniggered. "You can say that again, my friend."

The shambling group of survivors slowed down at the end of the corridor and the idiot curator turned to face them all. "Okay everyone, once we get inside we should barricade the doors right away. I don't think I need to tell you why." The man paused so that they could all listen to the banging coming from the door down the corridor behind them. Randall didn't appreciate the dramatics, but kept his silence as the man continued. "Once that is done, we can all do our best to relax while I try to contact the authorities."

No one spoke and Randall didn't blame them. What was there to say in a ridiculous situation like this? And to take orders from one of the men responsible for it made things all the more worse.

The curator pushed open the door at the end of the corridor and stood aside whilst people filed into the room ahead. Randall listened to the erratic thudding getting louder behind them. It was all very confusing.

Can lions behave like this? Smashing through doors to get at people after already devouring several bodies already? It can't be hunger.

The tattooed man beside Randall patted him on the back. "They best have a kettle in there, pal. I could kill a brew."

Randall took exception to being touched by the rough-looking gentleman, but even more to being called 'pal'. He didn't acknowledge his disapproval, however, because he was next in line to enter the staffroom up ahead. Randall stepped through into a large teal-carpeted room, featuring several sets of brand-new tables and chairs, several vending machines, two pool tables, and a modest kitchenette. The room was backed by a horizontal window that ran the entire length of the wall.

Is this what our money paid for? Somewhere for staff to laze about? Maybe they should have spent the money on better security for the animal enclosures. Then I wouldn't be suing them into bankruptcy.

Randall found a seat and placed himself down while the rest of the group seated themselves. It felt good to take the weight off his feet, gave him a chance to use his inhaler. It would not do to idle for too long, though, because he had somewhere important to be. The head of one of the China's biggest tire manufacturers would be waiting on him to discuss an investment in their UK strategy. It was just one more industry that the Chinks were planning to monopolise and Randall decided it was better to get into bed with them than to resist. It could cost Randall's company millions if he missed the meeting – and Black Remedy were not a firm that took kindly to incompetence. There was a long line of other investors eager to make the deal with the Chinese if Randall didn't. Lions or no lions, he had to get out of there.

I'll spare ten more minutes, then enough is enough.

The curator stepped into the staffroom along with his giant blond accomplice, the one who had been rude to Randall earlier. A young brunette girl and a small boy with a tatty backpack also accompanied them. He was pretty sure that the boy belonged to the blond man.

Probably an insolent little brat like his father.

The curator pushed the door closed and locked it, then turned to face the group. "This door is not especially heavy," he said, "so I think it would be wise to slide one of the pool tables in front of it. Do I have any volunteers?"

Yeah right! Randall scoffed. Don't expect me to start lugging furniture around for you.

There were a few volunteers but Randall paid them no mind. The only concern he had right now were the ticking hands on his Omega watch. Each second could be costing him money.

This will not do. We must wrap this up so I can get out of here.

Several minutes passed, the aimless fools just about managing to push one of the pool tables up against the door. Unbelievably, they had started playing a game on the other table.

What do they think this is? Break Time?

"Right!" The curator cleared his throat and addressed everyone once again. "Now that we have secured our safety, I should introduce myself. My name is Mason and I work here at the zoo. Unfortunately, I have no more knowledge of the current events than anybody else. I will, however, be going upstairs shortly to use one of the office phones to try and contact the authorities. Before that, might I ask if anyone has a cell phone?"

The group looked around themselves, but no one answered. Randall could have said 'yes', but he wasn't about to offer up his possessions to a bunch of fools.

Mason raised an eyebrow above his spectacles. "Really? No one has one? I thought the whole world had mobile phones these days?"

"Yeah," added a Black man with grey sideburns who looked a lot like Bill Cosby. He was holding up a piece of shattered plastic with various wires hanging out of it. "But mine got pretty bashed up during the attack, as you can see. I tried making a call, but the thing won't even switch on anymore."

The young girl spoke. "I had one in my bag. My bag is outside. I think we all just ran for our lives, without really thinking about our belongings."

Not me. Randall smirked. Too bad the rest of you are unorganised idiots. I made sure to keep a hold of my possessions.

Mason nodded thoughtfully and then shrugged. "A shame, but not much we can do about it now. Okay, I'll go try to find some answers for everyone."

"Make sure you find them in the next five minutes," said Randall, using the commanding tone that he had perfected throughout years of boardroom conflicts.

Mason sighed. "Mr Randall, I do not wish to do battle with you again. Please try to see-"

"No, you try to see how much you have caused us all an inconvenience. None of us should be sitting here right now, in danger, no less. You need to remedy this situation immediately – and I mean immediately."

"Yeah!" The agreement came from the bald tattooed man. "This has gone way beyond a bloody joke, pal!"

Mason sighed once more and Randall was sure that the man was defeated. "I implore you to be patient and in return I will do my upmost to get this situation resolved as quickly as possible. I can only do my best to make sense of things. For now the only place we know that is safe is here, inside this building. I'll go now and try to make contact with somebody in authority."

Randall relaxed back in his chair and smiled like a fox after dinner. "See that you do, my friend." Despite the curator's obvious skill in keeping a straight face, Randall could see tiny rivulets of irritation soaking into the man's expression. It pleased Randall.

"Afterwards," he added, "I would request that everyone give me their contact details. I will be taking this establishment to the courts and anyone that wishes to join me in that pursuit will be most welcome."

"I'm with ya, pal," the tattooed man replied.

"As am I," said a middle-aged woman with wispy grey hair and bifocals. "Someone has to be punished."

Randall couldn't help but grin. Splendid. Looks like I have a nice foundation for my case already. The more angry voices in a courtroom the better.

"Why you gotta be such a dick, man?" It was the Black man, standing by the pool table, cue in hand. "Can't you see the trouble we're in? People are dead and all you can think about is your damn self."

Who the hell does he think he is to question me?

"I live in a world where people are held accountable for their actions," said Randall. "Sorry if the notions of right and wrong are beyond someone like you."

The Black man scrunched up his face and stepped away from the pool table. "The hell that supposed to mean?"

Randall sighed. "Work it out, Cosby."

Before Randall got a reply, the large blond man entered the conversation. "Let's not pick at each other, okay? Mason has gone upstairs to make a phone call and shed some light on the situation. The rest of us should just keep ourselves occupied. Look," he pointed one of his giant arms across the room, "there's a television in the corner."

He was right, Randall noted. Perched on a pair of wall brackets at the far corner of the room was a brand new LCD TV.

Another extravagance Black Remedy paid for. Jesus wept!

"Okay," Randall conceded. "Television sounds like a good idea, but let's just put the news on. None of that daytime talk show drivel."

"Fine. No problem." The big large blond man bounded off towards the television set on legs that seemed more like stilts. The television was far away from where Randall was sitting, but big enough that he would still be able to see it.

When the blond man managed to find the remote and switch on the TV, it showed only a blue screen at first. After a couple of seconds of pressing buttons and flipping through several channels of empty static, a grainy picture finally appeared.

"The reception is really bad," said the blond man, "but I think I got the news. It's certainly not Jeremy Kyle."

"Yeah, it's a news report alright," Cosby added needlessly. "I recognise the journalist, Jane Hamilton."

Everyone sat quietly as the news updates flashed various images from around the UK. It seemed that it wasn't just the zoo that was having troubles.

"Holy shit!" Cosby cried out. "I can't believe it."

If Randall was honest, he couldn't quite believe it either. "Interesting," he said out loud, wondering what it could all mean. "Very interesting."

CHAPTER 5

JOE COULDN'T BELIEVE what he was seeing. The flickering news report showed animal attacks from several areas of the country – images of Regent's Park overrun by snarling dogs of numerous breeds and even more bizarrely, a pack of crazed squirrels attacking a baby in its pram outside Bristol's Clifton Cathedral. Next came scenes from the countryside – of farm animals ripping a man to shreds in Paignton as he failed to reach the safety of his dust-covered Range Rover. Sheep, cows, and even pigs were roaming the fields and roadsides like Nazi-death-squads, with what looked like morsels of human flesh hanging from their jaws. Every scene was different, but they all had one thing in common – animals were attacking people. It didn't matter how big or how small, anything with fur, claws, or fangs was seemingly possessed by a malevolent rage directed solely at the human race. Dogs, cats, and mice, to sheep, cows, and pigs – all were united in their quest to kill. Whatever was going on right now, it wasn't just isolated to the zoo.

"This can't be happening," said Joe, as the television switched to similar scenes from various locations in Europe. Helsinki was currently under siege from a band of rampaging bears, while Paris was fighting off a plague of rats emerging from its vast sewers. "God help us."

"I don't think God is watching," said Grace, who had picked Danny up into her arms to keep him from looking at the images.

Joe shook his head, unable to take his eyes away from the screen. "I don't understand any of this."

"Me either." The man with the grey sideburns came up beside them. "It's a mad house."

Joe somehow managed a smile. "What's your name? I'm assuming it's not Cosby?"

"Name's William, but my friends call me Bill – don't mention the coincidence to that stumpy guy in the suit. Your name's Joe, right?"

Joe nodded. "Pleased to meet you, Bill. You make sense of any of this?"

Bill shook his head. "Just about the craziest goddamn thing I've ever seen. Don't know what could be to blame. Maybe it's the end of the world."

"Terrorists, if you ask me." Coming to join them was the grey-haired woman that had spoken out in support of Randall earlier, wanting to join him in his legal battle. She was smiling now and seemed quite pleasant. "Godless monsters are always coming up with new ways to destroy the world. Looks like they finally came up with a good one – airborne rabies. Name's Shirley."

"Hi, Shirley," Joe greeted her. "You really think terrorists?"

"Have a better suggestion?"

Joe shook his head. He didn't. If it was a terrorist act, he wondered what that could mean, and what it would mean for his son. "What do we do?"

"How should I know?" Shirley shrugged. "Whatever happens, things will work out however God wants them too. Maybe the world will finally face up to its sins now that deliverance is upon us."

Bill huffed beside Joe. "Speak for yourself, lady. People are responsible for their own actions. I don't believe there's some man in the sky playing us all like puppets, weighing up our mistakes against us. That's crazy!"

Shirley smirked, but the expression contained a dose of venom. "Believe what you will, but when your day of reckoning arrives you will see the error of your ways. Now is not the time to be a heathen." The woman strolled away; apparently satisfied that she had said her piece.

Bill turned to Joe. "She for real?"

"Don't know," said Grace, "but that was a bit of an intense introduction."

"Mentally ill if you ask me."

Grace shook her head and seemed uncomfortable. "Being strange doesn't mean you're crazy."

Joe laughed. "Strange times call for strange people, I guess. It doesn't matter who, or what, is responsible at the end of the day. The only thing that matters to me right now is keeping my son safe. You think things will work themselves out if we just stay put?"

Bill shrugged. "The police must be doing something. Hell, the army too! It's just a bunch of animals. They should be able to handle a few rabid Labradors and Tabby cats."

"What about lions?" Grace asked.

"Lions are a little more difficult, but that's only because we had the misfortune to be at the mother-fuckin' zoo. I mean, damn, you couldn't make this shit up."

Joe winced at the language and motioned to his sleeping son.

"Sorry," said Bill immediately.

"So what's the plan?" Grace asked Joe, shifting Danny's weight onto her opposite shoulder. "Do we just stay here?"

Joe had no answers. He scratched at his forehead on the off-chance that he would knock loose an idea, but found nothing hiding. "I guess we just settle in and wait for help to come. It'll probably take time for the authorities to get a handle on things."

Especially if this is happening everywhere.

Just then a door swung open at the edge of the room, startling everybody. When it turned out to be Mason, they all relaxed. The zoo's curator ambled over with a look of grave concern on his face.

Joe nodded to him. "Everything okay?"

Mason shook his head and looked down at the floor. When he looked back up his expression seemed even grimmer. "I tried contacting the admin building, but got nothing. The phones just rang out. So then I called the police."

Joe cleared his throat, not sure he wanted to hear what Mason had to say. "And?"

"No answer."

Grace frowned. "What? No answer? They have to answer, don't they?"

Mason bit at his lip. "One would certainly think so, but I'm getting the impression that they may be inundated with calls right now."

Joe knew where this was going and didn't want to beat around the bush. "We just saw the news. It's going on all over the country. We saw it happening in Paignton and Bristol."

Mason rubbed at his jawline. "Interesting," he said. "Paignton and Bristol both have zoos."

Joe shrugged. "So do a lot of places. I don't think that has anything to do with it. Things are bad everywhere."

"Yes," said Mason. "I suspected as much. Every number I tried was unanswered. But what really disturbed me is what I saw through the upper-floor windows."

Joe took a deep breath which seemed to lead Bill and Grace to do the same. Maybe anxiety was infectious. He raised an eyebrow at Mason and asked the question. "What did you see?"

Mason didn't answer at first and seemed to drift off into thought, eyes flickering behind his spectacles as though they were playing back a movie in his mind. When he finally answered, his voice was weak and lacked his usual composure. "The entire zoo has been overrun. The animals are all out of their cages and there are..." Mason took a moment to gather himself. "There are bodies everywhere. I watched for ten minutes whilst the zoo's pack of African Wild Dogs ate the very flesh from a group of dead children. Blood every--"

Joe cut him off and pointed to his son. Danny didn't need to hear any of this. Hopefully he was sleeping soundly.

My incredible sleeping son. One way of dealing with the situation, I guess.

Mason understood the warning and changed his tone to something more positive. "Yes, well, perhaps it is best to think forward now that events have already transpired. I believe we are safe for now, but I have no idea how long we should prepare to be here. If I tell the group what has happened, and that we all must remain inside, I think they may kick up a fuss."

Bill laughed. "That's an understatement. Biggest problem is gonna be that jackass banker – or whatever he is."

"Christopher Randall." Joe sniffed. "He works for Black Remedy."

Bill's eyes went wide. "BR? Shit, ain't they the biggest company in the world? What are they doing at a piddly zoo like this?"

Joe shrugged. "They seem to have their name on a lot these days. I even think the cruise I took during my honeymoon was on a boat owned by them. It isn't that surprising that they invested in a zoo as well as everything else."

"Well, the guy's a jackass, whoever he works for."

Mason looked weary and seemed to have aged over the last hour. "We'll just have to do our best to calm him. I'm sure he's a reasonable man underneath."

They all looked at each other for a minute. Joe didn't think anybody believed that Randall was anything other than a grade-A prick.

"Should we get to it then?" Mason asked them all finally.

Everybody nodded. No time like the present to serve shit sandwiches to a bunch of scared people. Joe just had to keep reminding himself that they were lucky to even be alive right now. They had to be thankful.

Led by Mason, they moved over to the centre of the room. Most people were still glued to the on-going news reports, but when they noticed the zoo's curator, they all turned their attention to him.

Mason clapped his hands together. It was a needless action since all eyes were already on him, but seemed like an appropriate way to punctuate the start of a speech. "I'm sure everyone is eager to gain more knowledge about the current events and I do indeed have some for you. I ask that you remain calm as I say this, but I regret to inform you that the animal attacks we have witnessed here today are not localised to this zoo. In fact, from my estimation, they are happening throughout the nation."

"Thank you for telling us what we already know." Randall spoke from the back of the room. The way he lazed casually in the chair made it obvious that his ego wasn't yet ready to take a rest.

Joe eyeballed the piggish little man. Anyone would think that being a pain in the ass was his hobby.

"We already know it's happening everywhere," Randall continued. "It was on the news."

"Okay," Mason replied, stuttering slightly. "Then I hope you all understand the gravity of the situation. What you may not be aware of, however, is the danger presenting itself outside this very building."

Randall shrugged. "The lions?"

"I wish that were the depth of it, Mr Randall, but I am afraid it is far worse. From what I have witnessed, every animal in the park has broken free. They have attacked and killed anyone unfortunate enough to be outside."

Randall leapt up from his chair, quicker than one would have imagined for a man of his girth. For a moment Joe wondered if someone had lit a fire under his ass. "How the hell have you let this happen?" Spit flew from his mouth as he spoke. His cheeks turned red like cherry tomatoes. "How does a modern-day zoo let its entire inventory get loose? It begs belief that anyone could be so incompetent."

Mason only managed to respond with a series of splutters.

Randall continued his tirade. "Do you know how much trouble you are in, my friend? I ought to throw you out there with the lions. You ridiculous, negligent--"

"Enough," Joe cut in. "There will be a time for blame, but this is not it. Right now we are in a predicament beyond anything we can yet understand. I think it's safe to assume that whatever is happening at this zoo is a symptom of whatever has affected the animals nation-wide – not the cause."

Randall glared at Joe. "I don't know who you are, Beanstalk, but I am getting rather tired of you coming to this fool's aid. If you continue to speak in his defence then I can only assume that you are complicit in this fiasco."

Joe threw back his head and twisted the kinks from his neck. Every conversation he had with Randall left him exhausted. The man was like a verbal succubus.

"Look," Joe finally said, "my name is Joe. I came here today because my son loves animals and has never been to the zoo." He pointed at Danny who was still asleep in Grace's arms. "Truth be told, I don't get to see my son very often and this day was important to me. Real important. So don't assume, Mr Randall, that I'm not as put out as everybody else. But there are people outside that never even made it long enough to be stuck in this situation. They're dead." A silence filled the room and Joe hoped that things were finally sinking in. "We're in a bad situation here, people, and if we don't all get along then it will probably get even worse. It would be nice if we introduced ourselves and tried to get through this together. Is that too much to ask?"

More silence filled the room. Nobody wanted to talk. No one wanted to get along. To do so would be to admit that things were as bad as they all feared.

"My name is Grace. I'm twenty-three and I came here today for a job interview. I don't think I'm going to get it."

Joe smiled at her, appreciating her effort. "Anybody else?"

Shirley stood up from a chair behind Randall. "My name is Shirley. I'm a retired nurse and I come to the zoo often. It's only right that we appreciate God's creatures and enjoy the beauty of his creation. I do charity work for this zoo and for the Church of England."

The next person stood up: the bald man covered in red and green tattoos that wrapped his arms like sleeves. There was one stamped across his throat that read: HIGHLANDER. "Name's Victor," the man said in a thick Glasgow accent. "I were on a date. The wee gal died outside, I think. I only came the bloody zoo to please her. Waste o' bleeding money."

Joe was surprised that the man didn't seem particularly bothered by the death of his date. He supposed people grieved in different ways.

"I'm sorry to hear that, Victor. What has happened today is a tragedy."

"Ay, a tragedy." Victor repeated. "Woman had a damn fine backside."

The comment may have been a joke, but it elicited only a brief moment of awkward silence until the next person stood up.

"Hi, everyone. You can call me Bill. I'm a self-employed accountant. Came here today with my partner, Gary. He's dead too, I guess." Suddenly the man seemed very close to tears and his speech became very slow and considered. "I tried to help him, but..."

Victor threw his hands up in the air, letting them fall down and slap against his thighs. "Oh great, we're stuck in here with a bleedin' fairy!"

Bill waved an arm at him dismissively. "Oh great, we're stuck in here with a closed-minded bigot."

"What you say to me, faggot?"

"Sorry," Bill said. "Were you not intending to come across as a bigot? I kind of got the impression that you were."

Victor stomped towards Bill. His muscles bunched up and ready for a fight. "You don't get to call me anything, you hear me, bumboy?"

Joe got between the two men, towering above them both. "Pack it in! We don't have to like one another, but at least act like adults. Victor, you're out of order."

"Screw you, pal."

"Dad?"

Joe turned around to see that Grace had put Danny down and that his son was now walking towards him in a fuzzy, half-daze.

"Hey, sleepy head," said Joe. "Everything is okay. The adults are just talking."

Danny rubbed at his eyes. "Why are you shouting?"

Joe picked his son up into his arms. "I'm not shouting, buddy. I was just excited about something."

"About the monkeys?"

Joe frowned. "What monkeys?"

Danny rubbed at his eyes once more, before pointing over his father's shoulder. Joe turned around to see what his son was looking at. The others in the room did the same.

"Shit pickles," said Grace beside him. "That's not good, is it?"

Joe shook his head. "No, not good at all."

This really can't be happening.

Lined up against the horizontal window of the far wall was row upon row of monkeys. Dozens of human-like faces pressed up against the glass side by side. They looked almost comical in a way, but a wild spark of sinister intent glinted in their eyes. Joe knew what the glint represented.

It was murder.

CHAPTER 6

"**W**HAT DO WE do," Grace cried out, frantically pulling at her hair. "What do we do?"

Joe put a hand on her shoulder whilst simultaneously pulling Danny against his hip. "Just calm down," he said. "I don't think they can get in at us."

As if to question his assertion, one of the monkeys smashed a fisted paw against the glass. Joe flinched and studied the area where the animal had hit. It was cracked, a delicate spider web of fractures snaking through the glass where the impact had struck.

Joe swallowed. "Actually, maybe you should go ahead and panic."

"We need to move upstairs, right now." Mason rushed across the room, clapping his hands above his head to get everyone's focus. A door stood at the side of the room and he punched in a code on a square pad beside it. "Everyone, in here, quickly."

Without argument everyone raced to the door, passing through into the corridor beyond. Joe and Danny went in last, slamming closed the door behind them, hearing it lock automatically.

Mason was waiting for them. "We need to move to the second floor before they get in."

Joe's palms were sweaty and he wiped them against his jeans. "Will we be safe up there?"

Mason was already moving again. "Something tells me that we're not going to be safe anywhere."

Joe peered down at Danny, who was looking right back at him. Worry was etched across his delicate face and it made Joe's heart twist in his chest. He tussled his son's blond hair and picked him up onto his hip.

Mason shouted back and told them to hurry.

"Okay," Joe said. The sound of breaking glass from the staffroom urging him to get moving. He caught up with the rest of the fleeing group just as they reached a staircase at the end of the corridor. Footfalls echoed as Joe took the steps two at a time. More than once he almost lost his balance. Danny's limp weight in his arms didn't help.

At the top of the stairway was another lengthy corridor, carpeted in a cheap navy-blue pile and lined by numerous doors on both sides. Mason was leading everyone into the nearest door on the left. A bronze plaque on the wall beside it read: ZOOLOGICAL LIBRARY AND SEMINAR ROOM.

Joe stepped in beside Mason to find a plush area, full of soft furnishings, chairs, and wooden tables, all facing forward toward a lectern at the back of the room near a large ceiling-to-floor window. The other three walls were interspersed with overfilled bookshelves and recently-used whiteboards. The musty smell of freshly-inked pages filled the air.

"We need to barricade the door downstairs," said Mason, "make sure that nothing gets through into the corridor."

Joe swallowed a lump in his throat. "I don't fancy going back down there. It sounded like they were about to break right through the window when I started up the stairs."

The tattooed man, Victor, came over to them. "I'll go," he said. "Bunch of wee monkeys don't scare me none."

"That's very brave of you," Joe admitted.

"Aye, well it's not your fault you're a pussy."

Joe cleared his throat. "Excuse me? I have a son to look after first and foremost. I've already risked my life enough times today."

Victor sniggered and sauntered away, towards one of the room's many desks. "Keep telling y'self that, pal."

Joe shook his head and put his son down on one of the cushion-backed chairs, then took the seat next to him. I'm not a pussy. I just have other priorities right now. Although, if someone doesn't go down and barricade that door then we'll all be in trouble. Maybe I should go...

Victor dragged a table over to the doorway and the scraping sound against the thin carpet broke Joe away from his thoughts. He sat and watched the man grab a second table and upend it on top of the first, then drag them both into the corridor outside.

"Can this situation become any more farcical?" said Randall, complaining again and as upbeat as ever. "A total disaster!"

"Think I'd have to agree with you there," said Bill, rummaging through one of the bookshelves. "Things keep going from bad to worse."

"We should be okay for now, though," said Mason. "Victor is barricading the door as we speak and there's no other way to reach this section of the building other than the staircase we just ascended."

"Shouldn't someone be helping Victor?" Shirley asked.

"He can handle himself," said Randall. Joe was glad to hear it from someone else. "I'd be more concerned about your own hide and the situation we're in, my dear."

Bill returned a thick text book to its space on the shelf and turned around. "And what situation are we in exactly? I still don't know."

Grace offered an explanation. "I think things are...bad. I mean really bad. If this is happening everywhere then we could be in some serious trouble. There might not be anyone coming for a long time."

"That's ridiculous," said Randall.

"I don't think so," said Joe. "I'm sure everything will work out eventually, but I don't see anyone coming by to help us for a while. If animals are attacking everywhere then the whole country is going to be in chaos. I didn't want to admit it at first, but I think we're all stuck here."

Mason nodded. "We need to start thinking about settling in, planning for a couple of days here."

Randall slapped his hands down on one of the tables, startling everyone. "Unacceptable!"

Bill put a hand to his forehead. "Seriously, man, you gotta wake up. This shit is bad and it's time to forget about business appointments and brunch in the city."

"I need to get out of here. I am far too important to be missing in action. There are people who rely on me."

"Those people are probably dead," said Grace.

The suggestion seemed to hit home to Randall and he stood there silently, swaying back and forth slightly as his mouth moved in speechless quivers.

"I'm sorry," said Joe, "but that's most likely true. I think we're alone for now. We should just count ourselves lucky that we're alive."

"Count yourself lucky," said Randall. "I don't see it that way."

Joe put his hands up. "Fine, but can you at least accept the situation we're in?"

Randall said nothing. He moved away from the group and sat down. That was fine by Joe. The further away the piggish little man was the better. He leant back in his chair and looked at his son. "You've been a really good boy today, Danny. Very quiet and well behaved."

"The animals are after us, aren't they? They don't want to be in cages no more."

Joe thought about lying to his frightened son, but found that he couldn't. "Something has made them really mad at us," he admitted, "but I'm going to look after you."

"Promise?"

Joe smiled and said, "Ohhhh yeahhhhh!"

Danny laughed hard. "Macho Man!"

"That's right. Anything that tries to hurt you will get the big elbow drop."

Bill and Grace joined Joe and Danny at the table, attracted by the noise. "Everything okay here?" Grace asked.

"I was just telling Danny what a good boy he's been."

"You're telling me!" She patted Danny on the arm. "Not a peep out of this brave warrior."

Danny smiled. "Ultimate Warrior."

Grace looked at Joe, confused.

"One thing to know about my son is that he's obsessed with wrestlers from the eighties and nineties. I'm kind of hoping he'll get over it."

"Where did he get that from?"

Joe's cheeks flushed red. "Me."

Grace giggled. "Nothing wrong with that. Better than being football-obsessed like most the guys I meet. I'm surprised you never ended up being a wrestler yourself, size you are."

Joe looked at himself and nodded. "I think that's why I liked it as a kid. I was bigger than everyone else and I felt like a bit of an oddball, but every week I would watch these giants on TV being worshipped by millions and I wouldn't feel so bad anymore."

"Maybe that's why I used to like Culture Club," said Bill, and they all laughed.

Until the noise cut them off.

A ruckus somewhere in the building. The crashing sounds of a violent struggle. It wasn't until they heard the shrill shrieking of monkeys that it became obvious what was happening.

"Victor!" said Joe. "The monkeys must have broken in before he had chance to secure the doors."

Bill leapt up. "We need to get that door closed."

Joe sprang up too. "Grace, look after Danny. Danny, I'll be right back. Be good."

Joe and Bill swung open the door and ran into the corridor. The chaotic noise became louder as it echoed off the walls on their approach to the stairs. They could hear Victor screaming out insults.

"Take that, yer wee bastards! I'll break yer frickin' necks."

Joe took the steps downwards, twice as fast as he'd gone up them – four at a time – the impact of every stair rattling the bones in his ankles. Despite his haste, it still felt like an eternity to reach the bottom. When he did, with Bill hurtling into the back of him, Joe wished he hadn't.

The monkeys were inside.

Victor noticed Joe and Bill's presence and spun around to face them with his back against the door. Thick scratches and ragged bite-marks covered his body. "Give me a bloody hand, will ya!" he shouted.

Joe and Bill rushed forward down the corridor, gripping the edge of one of the tables that Victor had abandoned half way down. It was heavy and Joe wondered how on Earth the Scotsman had manoeuvred two at once. They slid the table towards the door, which was now being forced open by two-dozen sets of razor-tipped paws. Victor was pushing back as hard as he could, trying to force it shut, but there were four monkeys already inside the entranceway and they were all lunging for him. They bit and clawed at his tattooed arms and legs, shrieking in ecstasy as they drew fresh blood from his wounds. Victor ignored them and kept his concentration on keeping the door closed.

Joe's eyes stretched wide. The situation would not quite compute in his brain, but he knew that he needed to act right now, before Victor's body gave out to the relentless mauling by the four monkeys.

Joe prepared himself for battle. "Time to lay the smack down on your monkey asses."

He sprinted towards Victor.

CHAPTER 7

RANDALL DIDN'T KNOW who the hell they thought they were. *Talking to me like that. I could buy and sell the lot of them, yet they speak as though I'm no one.* He took a tug on his inhaler, enjoying the feeling of loosening lung tissue. *When all this is over, they will pay.*

Randall had been sitting and watching from his position away from the group for ten minutes now, looking out of the window that ran the entire length of the wall. The view outside was unusual, to say the least, but it lent credence to what the others had all been saying. Things were indeed bad.

The number of dead bodies scattered outside on the zoo's various pathways must have numbered fifty or more. There were slimy morsels of flesh littering the area like grizzly lawn ornaments. The numerous corpses wore grim expressions of agony, as though their final thoughts had been frozen onto their torn faces forever. It was all very interesting.

Obviously something fundamental in the universe had changed, gone off kilter. Only those willing to adapt would be able to cope with whatever lay ahead. Randall planned on being one of those people.

There will be heroes born of this situation.

The animals outside milled about with purpose and determination that should have been alien to lesser species. Grouping together, in what seemed to be a search and destroy mission, and sniffing out all corners for people who still lived – but there were no people left, as far as Randall could see, and their search seemed to be coming to an end. He watched curiously as a threesome of raggedy hyenas congregated next to what looked to be a pack of oversized housecats. There were many other creatures that Randall could not name, along with the many more obvious species that he could: animals like camels, zebras, and various species of deer. Wildlife had never been of much interest to Randall, and collecting animals together in a park, so that little brats could poke and prod at them, seemed pointless.

Better to just put them down than enslave them. Especially the dangerous ones. People must be mad to keep a bunch of lions around. Just look at the situation it caused today.

Randall lent over on his chair, tilting towards the nearest bookcase. He plucked a hardback book from the shelf and dropped his chair back onto four legs. There was nothing about this situation that Randall liked. He decided the best thing to do while he was stuck there was to learn a bit about the animals. Maybe then he could do something useful if they attacked again. He turned the first page of the book in front of him and started reading, oblivious to Victor's screams that had just started from the floor below.

CHAPTER 8

JOE COULD NOT believe he had just struck a monkey in the face. It had jumped up and clawed itself onto Victor's neck and was just about to draw blood when Joe wound up and threw a heavy right hand. The blow stung his fist, but it hurt the monkey more. The primate lay unconscious now, on the floor, twitching and staring up at the ceiling like a punch drunk boxer.

The other three monkeys were already taking its place and Victor kicked out at them as he struggled to keep the door from opening. "Get these bloody things away from me!"

Bill came up behind Joe, pushing the table in front of him. "You help Victor and I'll get this up against the door."

Victor continued to kick out at the monkeys in front of him. They hissed and swiped back at him with their blood-stained paws. Joe swung his leg at them, but they moved just in time and Joe found himself kicking his foot through thin air. He lost balance, swinging his arms to steady himself.

A monkey seized on the opportunity and leapt at Joe's arm as though it were a tree branch, clinging on with sharp-nailed hands and feet whilst at the same time wrapping its wiry tail around his bicep. Joe shook like crazy, but the animal stayed put, digging in even harder with its claws. Joe thought he might pass out from the pain, and only just managed to step aside as Bill came up fast with the table behind him.

"Out the way!" Bill rammed the table up against the door. Victor had to leap up and over it before it pinned him. Once on the other side the Scotsman helped Bill push the table tighter against the door.

Joe screamed out for help. "This thing is gonna rip my goddamn arm off!"

Victor stomped towards Joe, covered in his own blood and with a look of pissed-off determination on his face. He deftly dodged the other two monkeys that blocked his path and made straight for the third, the one wrapped around Joe's arm.

"Bloody oversized rats." Victor snarled and produced a menacing knife from somewhere on his person like he were performing a magic trick. "Time to get busy, Martha," he said to the blade, then casually slit the monkey's throat. The animal fell limply from Joe's arm, hit the floor silently, and quivered as blood streamed from its body.

Joe stumbled away, clutching his arm. Weeping gashes covered his flesh, but none seemed too deep to endure. He looked around the corridor and immediately spotted the other two monkeys who were still an active danger. "Quick," he shouted. "We have to get them."

Victor shoved Joe back, holding his knife out in front of him. "You two get back upstairs. Me and Martha can handle it from here, no bovva."

Joe went to argue, but Bill put a hand on his chest and eased him away. "Let's get your arm looked at. I don't have the stomach for this."

If Joe was honest, he didn't either. He avoided looking back as he made his way up the staircase. The wet stabbing sounds and animalistic shrieking was enough to turn his stomach inside out.

* * *

Joe couldn't stop shaking. Neither he nor Bill talked about what had just happened downstairs – how calmly Victor had brandished that knife.

Did he call it 'Martha'?

I should be thankful of the guy, Joe thought. He did what no one else could. Probably saved my arm. Still, would like to know where he got that knife from.

He must have been carrying it the whole time.

Joe had a bad feeling, but it wasn't worth worrying about for now. He re-entered the seminar room and sat down next to Grace. Danny,

Bill, and Mason were there also. Randall and Shirley sat away from the group – Randall with his head buried in a book. Shirley gazing out of the window. Joe placed his hand on top of Grace's. "Thanks for looking after Danny," he said.

She smiled. "I think he was the one looking after me. I was worried."

"Really," said Joe. "Worried about me?"

Grace's cheeks went red. "Yeah. Bill, too, of course."

Joe nodded. "Oh. Well, we're both okay, luckily."

"What happened down there?" Mason enquired.

"There were some of those monkeys that got inside."

"Crab-eating macaques."

Joe raised an eyebrow. "What?"

"They're crab-eating macaques. If they're the same ones that were at the staff room window, that is. Not usually dangerous, but a large group of them can get into a frenzy."

"Okay, well, these...macaques...had nearly gotten the door open when we got there. A bunch of them were already in the corridor. They were attacking Victor. Luckily we managed to get the door closed again. We secured it with some tables."

"What happened to the macaques that had already gotten inside?" Mason asked.

Joe glanced at Bill, who looked away sheepishly. Joe didn't feel the need to freak everyone out with the gory details or what Victor had done. "Well, erm...Victor sorted them out. Managed to grab them and throw them back through a gap in the door while we held it open a crack."

Grace was next to speak. "What's Victor doing now?"

Bill answered. "He's securing the door some more. Making sure it's nice and solid."

Everyone seemed satisfied with the version of events, so Joe changed the subject. "Do we have anything for my arm?" He looked down at Danny, who had put his head into his hands when he'd seen his father's blood. He lent forward and whispered, "I don't want Danny upset. The wounds look worse than they are."

Mason slid his chair back and stood up. "Of course. I apologise for the delay. I should be able to find a first aid kit in one of the labs."

"Labs?"

"Yes. We are in the zoo's research wing, after all. There are several laboratories for testing and examinations, as well as a veterinary surgery that is used to treat the animals. Unfortunately, none of the vets are here today."

Grace laughed. "Think we'll have to play doctors and nurses ourselves then."

Mason smiled back, but the gesture was strained. "Quite."

Joe watched Mason walk away and hugged his son around the shoulders with his uninjured arm. "I'm gonna be okay, buddy. Just a few scratches."

Danny didn't lift his head from his arms and Joe wondered whether he was sobbing. "How can you look after me," his son mumbled, "if you can't look after yourself?"

It hurt Joe to hear his son had such little faith in him, but it was probably warranted given the circumstances. Joe continued patting Danny on the back as he spoke. "Even heroes get hurt, buddy. How about when the Warrior had a curse put on him by Papa Shango? Or when Macho Man got bitten by a snake?"

Danny lifted his head slightly, then put it back down again. "Or like when The Model blinded Jake the Snake with his cologne?"

"Exactly," said Joe. "They all got hurt, but it didn't stop them, did it? I'm still fighting, and I'm still going to protect you."

Finally, Danny looked up. He gave a cheery smile but his young face didn't wear it correctly amongst the tears.

"Don't cry, Danny," said Grace. "Your dad is a hero. He's been saving people all day. Nothing will happen to you with him around. He's too big and strong."

Danny giggled. "Do you like my dad?"

Grace blushed.

Joe saved her the agony of answering. "Danny! Don't ask people questions like that."

"Sorry, Dad."

Joe tussled his hair. "Okay. No problem, buddy."

At that moment, the door swung open and Victor stepped through. He was no longer covered by blood except for the staining on his clothes. Everyone in the room was quiet, but he didn't seem to notice their reaction. "All done down there," he chirped. "Those hairy bastards shouldn't be able to get through any time soon."

Joe suddenly felt increasingly protective of his son in Victor's presence, but tried not to show it. "Great!" he said. "We all owe you one."

"How did you get the blood off you?" asked Bill, eyeing the man's multiple scratches.

Victor grinned, teeth showing like rows of daggers. "Magic!"

Bill frowned. "Huh?"

"I grabbed a fire extinguisher off the wall and sprayed myself clean. Stung like buggery, but luckily it was just scratches and nothing nasty."

"Same here," said Joe, examining his own shallow wounds.

Before anybody said anything else, Mason entered the room.

"Couldn't find a first aid kit?" Joe enquired when he noticed the man wasn't carrying anything.

Mason shook his head and seemed lost for a moment. "Huh? Oh, yes. I mean, no. I got distracted. I...I think you should all come and see this."

Joe stood up. Whatever Mason had seen was not going to be good news.

CHAPTER 9

"WHAT ARE THEY doing?" Joe looked around at the rows of cages that lined the laboratory on all sides. "They've gone insane!"

"No shit," said Victor. "Was that not clear to you, pal?"

Joe ignored the comment, mainly because he was so horrified by what he was seeing. Dozens of small animals, trapped within cages, were hurling themselves against the steel bars, screeching furiously as they bled and bruised. The noise was deafening, made worse by the incessant clanging of the bars being struck by frantic bodies. Worst of all was the smell of shit hanging in the air like a wet blanket.

"What are they doing, Dad?" Danny asked.

"I don't know." Joe studied the various species of frenzied rodents and small mammals. "I think you better go back to the other room with Grace while we figure this out."

Grace obliged without complaint and took Danny's hand, leading him back out of the room. Joe stepped further inside and joined up with the other men, who were already deep in conversation around an aluminium operating table in the centre of the room.

Bill was talking the loudest. "They're gonna smash their own skulls in just to get at us!"

"I know," said Mason, cringing as the intense racket grew even louder. "In fact I think some of the smaller animals are already dead."

Sure enough, Joe spotted a couple of dead rabbits in a nearby cage, skulls smashed in and leaking pink and grey sticky fluid. He swallowed, trying to stem the bile rising in his stomach. "What could cause them to act like this?"

Mason shrugged. "There is nothing in recorded science that could override an animal's instinct to survive – at least not on a mass scale. Even rabid dogs wouldn't smash their own skulls in a blind rage."

"Obviously something has caused this," Randall said. "You obviously just lack the required knowledge to explain it."

"I agree," Mason admitted. "I lack any knowledge of what could cause this."

Randall seemed smug. Joe felt like punching him.

"But so would any other person in my field," Mason added. "This defies explanation. I don't know of any virus or biological condition that would present in this way. Even rabies would not present on such a wide scale."

Bill sighed. "I think what caused this is irrelevant now. What we need to think about is how to defend ourselves. What do we know about this thing, so far?"

The group thought for a few moments. Then Victor said, "We know that they're after us. Those wee monkeys downstairs were single-minded in taking chunks out of my arse. Nay else mattered to them. Like they were possessed or something."

"Yes," said Mason. "It's quite clear from what we are seeing in this very room that the animal's instincts are being entirely over-ridden by the desire to attack us; even at the expense of their own well-being. Whether or not they are 'possessed' is a different conversation altogether though. What else do we know?"

"They're working together," said Randall. "I saw them from the window in the seminar room. They were moving in groups, searching for people. Even animals that would usually attack each other like wolves and those brown, spotty cats were working together."

Mason rubbed both hands against his pale face. "Lynx. The zoo has eight Canadian Lynxes. They would have been the cats you saw – and you're right, the wolves should have attacked them. It is most disturbing. It appears that the laws of nature no longer exist. The animal kingdom has lost its natural instincts and replaced them with one prime directive: extinguish all human life. We are now at the bottom of the food chain, hunted by all other species."

"Not quite." Bill was standing over by the cages. "Look."

Joe and the others moved closer to the cages and saw what Bill was pointing at.

Mason leaned forward and examined closer. "The birds!"

Joe nodded. "The birds aren't affected."

The two plump, brightly-coloured macaws were extremely agitated, but it was clear that they were not suffering from the same malady as the other animals. They were just normal, frightened birds.

Victor spoke up. "So whatever's happening isn't affecting the birds? Grand! That makes my day a whole lot better."

"Sarcasm aside," said Mason, "this bodes well for us. If this phenomena had affected avian species then we would surely have been doomed. There are hundreds of thousands of birds in the UK alone and there would be no way to defend against them. This is very good news."

Joe agreed. He didn't like the thought of being in a real life version of The Birds. "I wonder if any other species are unaffected." he said.

"I suppose time will tell," said Mason. "For now, we should close this room off. Just in case the animals get free."

"Fuck that," Victor said. "Let's euthanize the bastards."

"We will do no such thing! Many of these animals are endangered species."

"So what! They've gone feral."

"I will not allow it!"

Victor pushed Mason aside and pulled out 'Martha', shocking those that had not yet seen her.

"Victor!" It was Randall speaking.

Victor spun around. "What?"

Randall went and placed a hand on the man's shoulder. "We are all going to have to work together now, so if our good friend, Mason, wants to leave these animals...intact, then I believe it would be best to do so – in the interest of cooperation. We should not be brandishing knives."

That's weird, Joe thought. Maybe Randall's not a complete git after all.

Victor's face scrunched up. "If these things spring loose," he said, "you'll wish different."

"Perhaps," said Randall, "but for now these animals seem secure enough not to concern us. Put the knife away, my friend."

After a brief hesitation, Victor finally returned Martha to her hidden sheath behind his back. He glared at Mason. "These things get free and it'll be on your head."

Mason nodded and Victor stomped away, joined by Bill and Randall. Joe waited behind. "We should go too," he said to Mason, eying up the creatures rampaging inside their cages. "Maybe they'll calm down if they can't see us."

"I hope so. They only started acting up once I entered the room. They were silent prior to that." Mason clicked his fingers. "I almost forgot again. I need to get you a first aid kit."

Joe laughed. "My arm will be hanging off by the time I get a bandage."

Mason allowed himself to smile and walked across the room towards the far wall. Sitting atop a filing cabinet was a bright green box. Mason reached out for it.

Then recoiled and hissed.

Joe rushed towards him. "What is it? What happened?"

Mason clutched his hand against his chest. "Something just bit me!"

Joe skidded to a halt on the floor tiles. "Shit! What was it? What bit you?"

Mason's hand had started to bleed from two round puncture wounds. Red globules dripped onto the ground. "I don't know. Be careful."

Being careful was not advice Joe needed. He trod carefully towards the filing cabinet, ready to bolt at the first sign of danger. As he got closer, he could make out a delicate scratching sound from behind the first aid kit. Something was definitely there.

But what?

Joe looked around for a weapon – something that would put some distance between him and whatever hidden creature had bitten Mason.

"Over there." Mason pointed. "There's a set of steel tongs for holding hot materials."

Joe saw the implement and grabbed it off the nearby table. The long metal rod felt good in his hands, empowering him enough that some of his nerves faded away. He crept towards the filing cabinet. Positive that the scratching sound was becoming louder.

"What should I do?"

Mason came up beside Joe, still clutching his wounded hand against his chest. "I don't know. Just be ready. Whatever it is was small and quick. You may only get one chance."

"What happened to your views about euthanasia?"

"The bugger bit me."

"Fair enough." Joe prepared to attack. He held out the tongs in front of him and aimed them towards the first aid kit. "Ready?"

Mason nodded. "Ready."

Joe prodded the first aid kit and knocked it onto the floor.

Yikes!

There, amongst a stack of papers and a pencil pot, was a snarling brown ferret the size of an obese housecat.

Joe swung for the bleachers.

"Damn it!"

A miss.

The ferret leapt towards Joe, claws outstretched and ready to draw blood. Joe spun around and managed to sidestep. Mason ran in the other direction. Joe readied himself for another swing. "A bloody ferret? Seriously?"

"They were going to add them to the petting zoo," said Mason. "They had one up here to assess its temperament."

Joe swung the metal tongs again – missed – struck the hard tile of the floor, sending a tingling sensation from his wrist to his elbow. "I think its temperament is grumpy."

The elongated animal lunged at Joe again. This time it managed to get a bite-hold on his lower leg, thick incisors burying deep into the fatty flesh of his calf. He hollered in pain, poked at the rodent with the tongs, tried to grip and twist the animal's elongated body away from him.

"Jesus, this thing won't give in." Joe felt needle-like fangs burrowing deeper into his skin, scraping against bone.

He screamed louder.

Mason rushed forward and tried to kick the rat away, but the man's complete lack of athletic prowess was evident. His kick missed completely and he stumbled onto his knees in a tangle of his own cumbersome limbs.

With the thrashing rodent continuing to take a chunk out of his calf, Joe looked for an urgent solution. Attached to one of the desks was a gas valve, leading to a Bunson Burner. He hobbled over to it.

The burner turned on easily enough – Joe's memories of high school physics helped him through. The sudden flame licked about two-inches into the air. He turned the inlet valve and sent the flame another inch higher. Without hesitation, Joe pushed the tongs into the flame, heating the tips. The ferret continued to rip and tear at his flesh, but he had to bear it for just a few seconds longer. If this was going to work, he needed to wait.

The acrid smell of burning dust filled the air. The metal tongs began to turn red.

Joe waited a few more, unbearable seconds, until he could take the dizzying pain no longer, then he pulled the tongs away and carefully lined up the molten pincers on either side of the ferret's thrashing head.

He clamped the tongs shut.

The animal immediately released its grip on Joe's leg and screeched in a pitch so hellish that it hurt his ears. The noise sharpened as the tongs tightened. Eventually, the ferret's squeals weakened into breathless whimpers, fading away to total silence. The furry body went limp. Joe released the tongs, letting them, and the ferret, fall to the floor.

"It's dead," said Mason. "But you probably already new that."

Joe panted, struggled to get his words out. "Can I please...get... that first aid kit now?"

Joe's body collapsed onto the floor, spilling fresh blood onto the tiles.

CHAPTER 10

"I'T'S TIME TO start planning, my friends." Randall had perched himself down on the edge of a desk as he addressed those present in the room. "It took me a little time," he said. "I'll admit that now. But I've finally come to understand the situation we are in. It will take organisation and planning to survive. We all need to be moving in the same direction, scribbling on the same page."

Cosby folded his arms. "What do you suggest?"

"That we act now rather than later. We need to find food, blankets, water. The building needs to be secured – at least our part of it. A strategy has to be in place if we are to get through this together. We don't know how long rescue might take."

"Where do we start?" asked the brunette girl, Grace. She was young and attractive, if a little plain. Randall noticed that her fingernails were chipped. It made her look cheap – and so did the many faint scars that lined her arms.

One of those self-harming misfits by the looks of things.

Randall grinned at the girl. He intended to look charming. "We start in order of priority, my dear. We need to secure this floor as much as possible, windows as well as doors. Then we need to find food and water. Once we've got those we can concentrate on settling in and waiting for help. I think we should split into two teams." Everyone seemed to be in agreement, so he continued. "Victor, you take Bill and Shirley. I'll take Grace and Mr. Mason. That is, whenever he returns from whatever it is that he's doing."

"What about Joe?" Grace asked.

Randall thought about it for a moment before answering her. "I was assuming that he could actually look after his son for once. I know he seems to prefer that you look after him, my dear, but right now the group needs you."

Grace looked down at the little boy asleep in her arms. "I'll just look after him until his dad gets back, then."

"Where is the big lummox anyway?" Victor asked.

Cosby answered. "He stayed behind in the lab with Mason. I think they're bandaging his wounds up."

Randall sighed. "Let's hope he hurries up and makes some use of himself."

"I think Joe has proven himself on a number of occasions."

Victor sniggered. "Sounds like you wanna bum the guy? Big dumb blonds your type?"

"Screw you!"

"You wish, poofter."

Randall put a stop to things before they could go any further. Childishness was not of benefit right now. "Gentlemen, please remember that you will be working together. Try to behave like adults."

Victor put his hands up, a wide grin on his broad, cat-like face. "I'm just fooling around. He knows I don't mean it."

Cosby glared at the other man. "Yeah right."

Randall waved a hand dismissively. "Okay, you two take Shirley and begin checking for any areas that need securing. It wouldn't hurt to seek out weapons too. See what you can find."

Victor nodded and took off immediately. After a short while, Shirley and Bill followed after him. That left Randall and Grace alone.

Along with the brat, of course. *Where the hell is his deadbeat father gotten to? Maybe those animals have escaped their cages and torn him apart. One can only hope...*

Randall scolded himself for such an ill-natured thought. Such a harsh attitude was not the way to proceed in the current situation. A certain amount of tact would be needed. He sat down next to Grace and smiled. "I guess we should get started then, sweetheart?"

Grace frowned and Randall made a mental note: She doesn't like 'sweetheart'. Don't use it again. He smiled at her. "I thought we could check each room for a water cooler. Office buildings always have them, do you agree?"

"Okay. Should I bring Danny with us or find Joe first?"

Randall thought about it. Guess it couldn't hurt to come across as child-friendly. "Yes," he said. "We can take the little sprog along. Perhaps we'll bump into his father along the way."

Grace seemed confused. "Your attitude has changed."

"I think the stress of this situation affected me worse than I first realised. I'm prone to making harsh judgements. A defence mechanism, I guess."

Grace's demeanour softened and she nodded. "Okay. Let's get going."

"Great!" Randall stood up and offered a hand. "Wake the young man and we'll make a start."

Grace rubbed Danny's shoulders. "Time to wake up, honey."

The boy stirred slowly. Too slowly, and Randall became impatient. "Come on now, lad. We're going to go and find your father."

The boy opened his eyes and looked around in a daze. "Where's Dad?"

"We're going to find him now," Grace answered.

The boy nodded and finally woke up fully. Randall forced himself to smile. "That's a good lad. You hold on to Grace's hand now, you hear?"

The three of them headed for the door and stepped out into the corridor. Randall couldn't be certain, but he thought he could still hear the riotous shrieking of the monkeys downstairs. Not to mention the rattling cages in the lab up ahead. He wondered if Joe and Mason were still inside.

"We should check the lab," said Grace, obviously wondering the same thing he was. "They're probably still in there."

Randall nodded. He put a hand out in front of Grace to stop her. "I'll go, but you stay here just in case there's any danger."

The boy whimpered and Grace stroked his head. "Daddy is okay, honey. We just need to check that there's nothing a little boy like you shouldn't see."

"I'm not little. I'm big and strong like the British Bulldog."

British Bulldog? The kid has a screw loose.

Randall didn't have time for this. "Wait here," he said. "I'll be right back."

He padded along the blue carpet and headed for the door. When he got there, he placed a hand around the long silver handle. Thoughts filled his mind about what he might find inside. His earlier notion of the animals escaping their cages now seemed quite plausible. The image of Joe and Mason ripped to shreds and lying in a pool of their own blood filled his mind. He almost turned back, but he had to do this, or else he'd lose face in front of the girl.

Slowly, Randall pushed down the handle.

When the door opened, the hinges squeaked. Randall hoped it wouldn't alert anything dangerous to his presence.

There was chaos inside the room. Randall immediately saw trails of blood – and what seemed to be a dead ferret. Amongst it all was Mason, kneeling over the body of Joe.

Is he dead? What the hell happened in here?

Randall was just about to burst into the room and offer his assistance, but he quickly reconsidered. Instead, he closed the door quietly and turned back into the corridor.

Grace was looking at him expectantly. "Well?" she asked.

Randall shook his head. "No one in there. They must have gone somewhere else."

Grace bit at her lower lip. The gesture suggested vulnerability and made her more attractive. "Why would they have gone someplace else?"

"I guess we'll know when we find them."

"We should probably keep on, then."

"Yes," said Randall. "Let's go see what else we can find."

CHAPTER 11

THE PINPRICK OF light gradually widened until Joe's vision returned. He found himself staring at the ceiling, his head throbbing like a drum beat, but the worst pain was in his leg. It felt like it was being held over a flame.

"Are you okay?" asked a voice from somewhere in the room.

Joe didn't reply for a few moments, and at first didn't even know who the other person was. Then, as he continued staring at the blank white ceiling and listening to the chaotic sound of rattling cages in the room, everything came flooding back.

He tried to sit up, but Mason held him down. "Wait a few minutes. Catch your breath."

"The animals, they've gone mad. I need to find Danny."

Mason shushed him. "Danny is fine. He's with Grace. You've been out for almost ten minutes."

Joe remembered passing out because of the pain. "My leg? How is it?"

"I think you'll be okay. You've got a pretty deep gash, but I stopped the bleeding. I bandaged it while you were out. Your arm too."

Joe examined himself and allowed himself a small laugh at the absurdity of what he looked like – a mummy in training. "I feel like a train hit me."

Mason smiled in a reassuring manner. It was surprising how much the curator's dry personality and lack of social skills could still be such a comfort. "No, it was just a little ferret. You certainly have been in the wars. Come on, I think you're okay to get up now."

Joe took Mason's arm and heaved himself up onto one knee. After a couple of laboured breaths he struggled to his feet. Pain stabbed through the bite-mark on his right thigh, but he fought it to the back of his mind. He had to get back to Danny.

"Easy there," said Mason, steadying him.

"I'm okay. Let's just get out of here."

The two of them headed back out into the corridor and crossed over to the other side. Mason opened the door to the seminar room and stepped inside. Joe followed, limping and wincing.

"Where is everyone?" Mason asked.

Joe's stomach rolled and a lightning spark shot up his spine. "Where's Danny? Where's my son?"

"I'm sure it's nothing. Let's just go look for them before jumping to any unhelpful conclusions."

Joe clenched his giant fists and felt himself tremble. They had no right to move Danny without informing him first. He stormed out of the room. If it were not for the agony in his leg he would have run.

"Slow down," Mason shouted from behind him.

But Joe did the opposite. He sped up, zigzagging the corridor from door to door and checking behind each one. Every room was empty.

"Danny!" he shouted.

Somewhere up ahead, a voice shouted back. Joe finally managed to run, ignoring the pain in his leg. Up ahead on the left was a room with the label: WAREHOUSE MEZZANINE.

"Dad, I'm here."

Joe pulled down the handle and pushed open the door. Inside was a cavernous room that stretched down to an open space at ground-level. It looked like a storage space for the zoo, a warehouse full of random crates and boxes. Joe was standing on a metal walkway that towered above. It led to a flight of stairs on the right and a small, win-dowed cubicle-office on the left. Danny was inside the office.

Randall was with him.

"Son of a bitch!" Joe sprinted into the office just as Randall turned around to face him. The punch caught the man square in his flabby jaw, knocking him to the floor. Joe stood over him. "What the hell are you doing with my son?"

Randall scooted back on his rear and rubbed his chin. "Are you insane?"

Joe noticed his son, shaking in the corner, and put an arm out. "Danny, come here."

Danny ran over to his father, buried his face in his stomach, and wrapped his arms around him. Joe turned his stare back to Randall. "Why were you alone with my son?"

"He wasn't alone," said a voice behind Joe.

He turned around to find Grace coming up the metal staircase from the warehouse floor. He raised his eyebrows at her. "What?"

Grace was shaking her head and seemed angry. "I told Danny to wait in the office with Randall while I looked downstairs for supplies. He wasn't doing anything wrong."

"Why did you all run off without telling me? What was I supposed to think?"

Grace laughed. It was an unpleasant sound. "You were the one that ran off. We didn't know where you were. We were hoping we'd find you on our way."

"What?" Joe stepped towards her, shaking his head. "You couldn't have looked very hard. I was still in the lab."

Grace seemed confused for a moment and Joe caught her glancing past him towards Randall. "But we looked there," she said. "Randall said the room was empty."

Joe turned around. Randall had gotten back to his feet and had plonked himself down on an office chair. The man was rubbing his chin and wheezed slightly as he spoke. "It was empty. It was a bit of a mess in there, but I didn't see you."

Joe didn't buy it, but, before he had chance to say as much, Mason came up behind and placed a hand on his back. "You were unconscious, Joe, and I was kneeling on the floor. It's quite possible that he didn't see us."

"Right," said Randall. "I only poked my head in – granted – but it looked to me like the room was empty. I'm very sorry, my friend."

"No," said Grace. "It's Joe that should be apologising to you."

Everyone looked at Joe and he suddenly felt like a misbehaved child. Reluctantly he accepted his error. "I'm sorry, Randall. I...acted badly."

"Yes, you did." Randall offered his hand out. "But we have bigger fish to fillet right now so let's just forget about it."

Joe couldn't be certain, but he thought he saw the beginning of a smirk on the other man's face. Still – whether he trusted Randall or not – Joe was the one in the wrong. "I'm sorry," he said begrudgingly.

"Okay then," said Grace. "Now that we've got that sorted, maybe Mason can tell us what's what in here."

"Of course," said Mason. "This is the zoo's storage warehouse. It's one of the places we keep dry animal feed, maintenance and landscaping tools, cafeteria supplies, et cetera. The cleaner's station is also here"

"Cafeteria supplies," said Grace. "Excellent, that's just what we need."

"Should we leave it here or gather it up?" Joe asked.

"I think it would be best to split it," Randall said. "If something happens to one stockpile then we will have a backup."

"Good idea," Joe admitted, although he hoped the theory wouldn't have to be tested. "Mason can show me where the supplies are and then we'll bring some of them up. Where are we gonna camp out with the stuff?"

"I think we should remain in the seminar room, for now," said Mason. "It's the only room with soft furnishings and it's the closest to the stairwell, which will give us the quickest warning if anything gets through the barricade in the lower hallway."

"Sounds like a plan," said Randall. "I'll check on Victor and the others and bring them up to da--."

They all heard the shouting from across the corridor. Two male voices. Neither of them happy.

Joe shook his head and sighed. "I think maybe we should all go and check on them."

CHAPTER 12

THERE WERE HUMANS inside. He could smell their wretched fear. They hid inside their tower, their symbol of comfort and fearlessness. While he had spent his life inside a cage, held back from the world by unrelenting bars, the humans enjoyed a freedom that should have been a right of all living beings. The humans had taken his freedom away many years ago, but now he was going to take it back. He was going to take it back for every creature enslaved by man. Something had happened. Things had become unquestionably clear. Things that he had once not understood were now simple concepts that he had learned without even being aware of how. His mind had changed – he was no longer an animal content to be enslaved.

The human's time as masters was over. There were underserving even to be slaves. They deserved only to be extinguished.

He roared and assembled his troops.

* * *

Joe and the others found Bill and Victor arguing in a cramped office at the end of the corridor. The conversation was heated and both men looked ready to get physical. Shirley stood nearby and seemed content to watch them.

Bill squared up to Victor. "Call me that again. I'm begging you."

"I think once was enough for you to get the point, pal."

"I'm not your goddamn pal."

Joe got between the two men. "What's happened?"

Bill took a step back and seemed like he was trying to keep hold of himself. "Man here called me a queer."

Joe looked at Victor, shocked that the man was grinning with what looked like pride. "Is that true?"

Victor nodded. "What's the problem? That's what he is, so where's the harm in being honest about it?"

"You're vile," said Grace.

Victor shrugged. "Your opinion, lass."

"Actually," Mason added. "I think you'll find that it's all decent people's opinion. It is wholly unacceptable in this day and age to use language like that."

Victor stiffened up defensively. "Where I come from we call a spade a spade."

Randall stepped up to Victor and pulled him slightly aside. "But you're not there now. You're here, and need to respect other people's feelings. When this is all over you can go home and think and say whatever you like."

"I'll think and say what I want where I want."

Bill slapped his hands to his forehead. "I can't believe I'm stuck with this homophobic fool."

"Look," said Joe. "If you want to keep making yourself unpopular, Victor, then go right ahead. The rest of us will just ignore you for the closed-minded jerk that you are. What I want to know is why the hell you two got into this in the first place."

Everyone took a breath and seemed to calm down for a moment. Bill finally answered the question. "We saw something from the windows and I panicked. That's when Victor decided to insult me."

"I just told you to calm down."

"What you actually said was, 'Calm down, queer.'"

Joe sighed.

"What did you see from the window?" Grace asked.

All of the anger in Bill's face drained away momentarily, anxiety replacing it. "I think it will be better if you look for yourself."

Joe nodded and Bill led the way as everyone followed over to the window. It was covered by a cheap venetian blind filmed in a layer of grey dust. Bill pulled at a drawstring beside the window and the shutters turned, casting dim shafts of light through the gaps. It was getting dark outside.

Joe walked up to the window and looked outside. He wished he hadn't. Gathered on the zoo's pathways was probably every animal in the park. They loitered in tightly-ordered columns, like a well-trained army from the nineteenth-century. Each species was grouped individually: A pack of Timber Wolves sat on their haunches in a rigid, three-by-three square; five giraffes stood together like the dots on a dice – four corners and a centre; a mother orang-utan crouched in front of her three adolescent offspring; the zoo's pair of komodo dragons flicked their tongues back and forth beside a small group of blood-soaked Meerkats, who themselves were stood next to a growling panther. The entire scene was an exercise in the impossible and there, amongst the entire battalion, standing almost exactly in the centre, was a lone silverback gorilla. Its massive size and strength was apparent even at a distance.

Their leader?

Grace had come to stand beside Joe and was now looking intently at the scene below. "What do you think they're doing?"

Joe could think of only one reason: "They're preparing for war."

"Impossible," said Mason, taking in the view himself. "Animals lack the necessary level of rational thought to behave that way. They behave on instinct not forethought. They cannot plan, they cannot strategize."

"I think the rules have changed," Joe said.

"If the animals are planning then we need to do the same," said Randall. "We need weapons."

"I agree," said Grace, "but let's not get ahead of ourselves. We can't be certain that they're assembling to get inside here. They could be preparing to leave the zoo."

Shirley cackled, getting everyone's attention whether she intended to or not. "They will not leave. Not while the damned and the sinful still fester among us."

Joe sighed and rubbed at his eyes. He was getting tired of a lot of things today but Shirley's preaching was high on the list. "What is happening has nothing to do with God. Even if it did, who are you to act like an authority? Who are you to label any of us as damned?"

"I'm not," said Shirley. "The Bible is our authority and it is He who condemns the damned. A man should not lie with another man."

Bill almost jumped in the air. "Not you too? What the hell did I do to deserve this? If it isn't Victor one minute, it's her the next. I can't be doing with any more of this shit."

Bill stomped away, but a smash against the window made him stop and turn back around. "The hell was that?"

Joe didn't know. Through the window he could still see all of the animals lined up in formation. Only one of them had moved – the silverback gorilla. It now stared straight up at Joe as if offering some unspoken challenge. There was something in its hand. A large stone.

Joe managed to duck to the floor just as the window shattered into a thousand jagged pieces. "He's throwing rocks!"

Grace leapt to the floor beside Joe, pulling Danny down with her. "Who is? Who's throwing rocks?"

Everybody hit the ground as another boulder flew through the broken window.

Joe scooted up against the wall. "The motherfucking gorilla, that's who. He's lobbing rocks like a Russian shot putter."

"Don't swear, Dad."

"Sorry, Danny. I'm just excited."

Grace stared at Joe, wide-eyed, brow-wrinkled. "Guess that answers our question about whether they know we're in here or not."

"Sure does, but as long as they don't get in I can live with a little bit of stone throwing."

"Joe!" Mason was calling him and pointing to something on the floor. The object was mottled grey with darker patches in several places.

A human head. Stripped of all flesh.

"I think it's more than just stones," said Mason.

Joe got up into a crouch and hurried his son and Grace away from the window. "Let's get out of here, everybody."

No one argued and the group hurried out of the office, regrouping in the corridor. They gathered into a disorganised huddle and Randall took the lead. "We need to find weapons," he said. "I think it's pretty obvious that they're not going to stop until they find a way in here. They'll climb the bloody walls if they can. We need to be ready when that happens."

"What weapons, though?" asked Bill. "It's not like we have guns and stuff."

"We don't need guns," said Victor. "We can improvise. Anything heavy or sharp will do. Plus we can set traps."

"Like in Home Alone." Danny smiled and seemed happy with his contribution.

"Yeah," said Victor. "Just like in Home Alone, little man."

Danny giggled. All things considered, he seemed to be holding up better than any of the adults.

Joe had a thought. "Hey, Mason, doesn't the zoo have tranquiliser guns? You see them all the time on television."

Mason frowned. "There are dart guns in the Ranger's station, of course, but I'm afraid that's at the other end of the zoo. There's another one inside a locked cabinet in the elephant enclosure, but again we'd have no chance of getting there. In the case of a severe emergency such as this, the local police force is trained to deal with escaped animals with lethal force. Our protocol would simply be to call them – which I have tried already.

"So there's nothing at all here to help us?" asked Bill, seemingly close to an emotional breakdown. He was rubbing at his forehead with both hands.

"There are drugs in the various laboratories," Mason added, "but the only way to administer them is by injection or oral ingestion. Does anyone want to get close enough to that gorilla to stick a syringe in him? I don't."

Joe showed his disappointment. "Okay, well then do you have any other suggestions for what we could use as weapons?"

Mason thought about it. "There will probably be certain items in the warehouse area. There's brooms, mop handles, et cetera. We could also look for the litter pickers that the Janitors use. They're long metal sticks with sharp spikes on the end."

"Like a spear," said Victor. "Bill should know how to use one of those."

Bill ignored the racist remark and Joe admires the man's self-control. Despite Victor being such an asshole, it was good news about the litter spikes. "That sounds like the best thing we have."

"Let's get going then," Randall urged.

"Should we split up or--"

The sibilant shattering sounds of more objects being thrown through the window of the nearby office alerted them all. It sounded like several things in quick succession.

"Do we ignore that?" said Grace. "Or do we look?"

Multiple rage-filled screeches sent Joe over to the door. Looking inside the office was probably a stupid thing to do, but he needed to know what they were up against. They couldn't afford to ignore a single thing.

Carefully, Joe cracked open the door and looked inside the room. There was movement inside. Lots of it.

You got to be kidding me?

White and black lemurs leapt about everywhere, flying in through the broken window, one after another. The small, bushy-tailed primates spotted Joe and immediately rushed towards him.

Joe slammed the door and pulled up the handle to engage the catch. When he turned back towards the group he didn't quite know how to explain it, other than saying: "We're under siege."

CHAPTER 13

"**T**HEY'RE COMING IN through the window," Joe told them. Randall shook his head in obvious confusion. "What are?"

"A bunch of those little monkeys – lemurs, I think. The ones with the ringed bushy tails and little hands? They've gotten into the office."

As if to validate his claims, several bodies hit the other side of the door. Sharp fingernails began to scratch at the wood.

Grace looked worried. "Do you think they will get through?"

Joe watched as the door handle rattled and then began to turn. He lunged for it and pushed it back up again. "Pretty sure, yeah."

"We need to jam the door," said Victor. "Somebody find something we can use to wedge the handle."

Grace stared at him like a deer in headlights. "Like what?"

"I don't know, woman, but the longer you stand there having a stroke, the longer it will take you to find something. Now get moving, you daft bint."

Grace rushed off. Joe hoped she found something soon because his fingers were already beginning to ache from clutching the door handle so tightly. The force on the other side was getting stronger and his grip was getting weaker. It was almost as if the diminutive creatures on the other side were infused with the strength of animals three-times their size. Joe didn't want to think about what that could mean. "I don't know how much longer I can hold this..."

"Just hold in there, pal." Victor tried to get a hold on the handle too, but there was no room for the both of them. Joe thought about changing with Victor, but the brief moment his hand would be off the handle could be all the lemurs needed to get the door open.

Grace reappeared in the corridor, holding a mop and bucket.

Victor laughed. "Clean up on aisle six, love? How's that going to help?"

Grace didn't say anything. She yanked the mop from the bucket and ran at Joe and Victor. For a second Joe thought she was about to brain one of them, but instead she shoved the wooden pole up against the door.

Joe realised what she was doing and watched in admiration as Grace threaded the pole behind the handle, twisting it so that both ends wedged against the door's frame on the left and right. Hesitantly, Joe released his grip on the door handle. It moved slightly, and for a split-second it looked like the plan might fail, but then the handle caught against the pole.

It held.

Joe shook his crippled hand, trying to get some feeling back into it. The knuckles ached as he flexed them. "Good thinking. I don't think I could have held on much longer."

Danny put his arm around her. "You're smart and pretty like Miss Elizabeth."

Grace raised her eyebrows at Joe.

Joe laughed. "She was a very famous lady in wrestling. It's a big compliment in Danny's world."

Grace knelt down and gave Danny a kiss on the cheek. "Thank you!"

Danny rubbed at the spot where she had kissed him and pulled a face. "Keep your lips to yourself, lady."

Joe was surprised to see everyone laugh at this, even Victor and Randall – although something about Randall's expression seemed a little forced.

The banging and scratching on the office door suddenly stopped.

"Perhaps they're giving up," Grace suggested.

Joe nodded. "Perhaps. Or maybe they're moving on to plan B."

"Plan B?" said Grace.

Joe nodded. "Something tells me that things are just getting started."

"All the more reason to commence with our own plans," Randall said. "We need to get moving, my friends. The quicker we can hunker down, the safer we'll be."

Everyone agreed. They had to do something proactive instead of waiting for the next attack. Joe had to keep his son safe no matter what. "I'll go look for the litter pickers in the warehouse," he said. "Grace, will you and Danny come with me?"

"Of course. I think I may have even seen where they were earlier."

"Excellent," said Randall. "I, and the rest of us, will gather supplies into the seminar room."

With the lack of any argument the group got moving. Joe, Grace, and Danny re-entered the supervisor walkway of the warehouse. Joe leaned over the safety rail and looked down over the various pallets on the floor below. "It's a bit of a maze down there."

"I know, but I think I saw the litter pickers over by the delivery shutter on the far wall."

Joe took his son by the hand. "Let's go down and get them then. Danny you stick close to Daddy, okay?"

Danny nodded and squeezed Joe's hand tight.

From the bottom of the steel staircase the warehouse seemed even more like a maze. Joe examined the first stack of pallets in front of him. It was full of cleaning products and housekeeping chemicals. It wasn't what he was looking for right now but Joe made a mental note of the various bleaches and the FLAMMABLE signs that adorned their bottles.

Grace stood behind him and placed a hand on his shoulder. "Anything?"

"I don't think so. Let's keep going."

The three of them moved on through the warehouse, cataloguing useful items, such as a pallet of canned cafeteria food and a small supply of petrol, while disregarding un-useful items like a crate of plastic animal souvenirs, although Joe did allow Danny to take a Rhinoceros from the pile.

Grace pointed. "I think they're over there."

Joe looked across the warehouse and saw a collection of metal rods stacked up against a steel shutter door. He walked over and grabbed one of them. After examining it he saw that it was indeed a spike-tipped litter picker. "Great," he said, thumbing the sharp point. "These will come in handy."

"How many are there?" Grace asked. "There're seven of us."

Joe sighed. "Only three, but it's a start."

"Sure is. Hopefully we won't need any of them."

Joe handed one of the spikes to her. "Better to be safe than sorry."

Grace looked at the tip of the spike in her hand and suddenly began to well up with tears. She wiped at her cheeks with her free hand. "I'm sorry. I just can't believe what's happening."

Joe put down the other two litter pickers and put his arm around her. "It's okay. We'll be fine. Whatever has caused this may well end soon. We don't know what's going to happen yet."

Grace squeezed into him, pulling Danny into the hug as well. "I'm so frightened. Things haven't even sunk in yet and I already feel like I'm going to have a breakdown. I saw people die today and I'm scared. Not just of the animals either."

Danny started crying also and Joe felt himself wanting to do the same. He couldn't allow himself to, though, because he needed to be strong for his son – maybe for Grace, too. "I'll look after you both," he said, hoping he was strong enough for it to be the truth. "We just need to stick together until all this is all over."

Grace pulled away and looked at Joe. Her eyes were red. "What if it's never over?"

Joe thought about it and didn't like what came. If the situation went on permanently then what hope was there?

"I don't know," he eventually said. "We just have to be ready – ready for whatever comes. Right now that means arming ourselves to the teeth."

Grace laughed and wiped at her face. "I guess we better keep searching then."

Joe grabbed the litter pickers back up and held them out like spears. "And if you see anything with fur, stab it!"

"Don't worry," said Grace. "I've given up being an animal lover. Time to bring out my inner-caveman."

A deep bass-filled bellow shook the warehouse and the three of them spun around with a start.

Standing twelve-feet away, poking out from behind a stack of spare plastic seating was an alligator. It was stretching its head into the air and raising itself up as if to show as much of its body as possible. After one more almighty bellow the creature lowered back down and stared at them with its ancient eyes. Then it hissed.

Grace moved up against Joe so that they were touching. "This thing doesn't have any fur, should I still stab it?"

Joe nodded. "I think it qualifies as something we should stab, yes."

The alligator came at them without warning, surprisingly quick for such a heavy animal. Its head swished back and forth as it approached them, jaws open, ready to taste human flesh.

"Get upstairs," said Joe. "I'll deal with this."

Grace shook her head. "No way. We should all just run for it."

"We can't abandon these supplies. We've got no chance without them. Plus we need to find out where this thing got inside, or else we'll have the whole zoo in here before long."

Grace hesitated, but as the alligator got closer she was forced into action. She ran, taking Danny with her and leaving Joe alone.

Joe sprinted away, too, but further into the warehouse instead of towards the stairs. "Come get me, you sad-excuse for a crocodile."

The animal followed Joe. He could hear it hissing and grunting behind him. He had no idea what he planned to do, but he was confident of outrunning the creature that was built more for water than for land.

Can't outrun it forever, though.

Joe stopped and spun around, litter spike in hand. The alligator was gone from sight, but still somewhere close by if the sound of its angered grunting was anything to go by.

"Hey there, alligator, where ya hiding?"

As if in answer to his question, the alligator lunged out from behind some boxes, taking Joe by surprise. The giant lizard crashed down on top of him, as heavy as a car. All of the wind was crushed out of Joe's lungs and stars clouded his vision. The only sense still operating coherently was his smell, which was picking up the fetid smell of half-consumed flesh coming from the creature's mouth.

Joe thought fast as the alligator wrestled to keep him pinned, trying to position itself well enough to get a clear bite at him. Thoughts of evenings alone, watching the Discovery Channel, suddenly entered Joe's mind and spurned him into action. In a bear hug, he wrapped his arms around the alligator's jaws, clamping them shut. Joe remembered that the muscles used to snap an alligator's jaws closed were exceptionally strong, but the ones that opened them were very weak. Joe held on for dear life, keeping the deadly maw closed.

It wouldn't keep him safe for long though. The crushing weight of the alligator was still immovable, and although he was strong enough to hold its jaws closed, eventually his stamina would give out and his arms would fail. He was doomed. His arms were already weakening, their strength ebbing away...

The beast thrashed about on top of him, fighting back against the grip around its jaws. Slowly but surely, the jaws began to open and Joe's arms began to part.

No more strength left, Joe released his grip. Clenching his eyelids shut, he waited for a death grip around his throat.

But none came.

Joe opened his eyes to find Grace standing over him. She had driven her litter picker into the skull of the alligator and was twisting violently, penetrating deeper into the creature's thick armour.

Without thinking, and acting entirely on instinct, Joe reached out to his side and grabbed his own litter spike from where he had dropped it on the ground. He pulled the weapon toward him, angled it at the soft flesh of the alligator's underside, then thrust with all his might.

The litter spike went all the way through the creature's head, poking out the top of its head like a horn. After several seconds of frantic convulsions, the creature flopped forward and went still.

From beneath the animal's bleeding corpse, Joe looked up at Grace. "You fancy making a handbag?"

Grace laughed, but was pale and shaken. "Maybe I'll make some shoes. Now stop messing around under there and get up, will you! We need to get this place secure."

CHAPTER 14

THINGS ARE LOOKING up, thought Randall.

They'd managed to find several full water coolers as well as a pack of cola cans in a mini fridge. Victor and Bill had found several heavy-duty office printers and dragged them downstairs to reinforce the barricade. Most of the windows on the upper floor were now blocked with upturned tables and filing cabinets. The remaining furniture had been piled up into the corridor at one end to stop anything getting through if the downstairs barricade was breached. All in all, Randall was quite pleased with the last hour's work. They would all be safe and his organisational skills were to thank for it.

These people owe me.

"That's it, Shirley," he said. "Just put anything useful you've found into a pile over on that table."

"Things are quite secure now," said Shirley, placing down a half-empty bottle of Evian amongst the other supplies. "I'm impressed that you've gotten things so well in hand."

"Thank you, Shirley. We can't afford to lose our heads in situations like this now, can we?"

"Not at all. It's good to see that we have such a strong man leading us."

Leading? Randall liked the sound of that. Shirley was obviously an astute woman that recognised his superiority amongst the group. "Thank you," he said again. "It's just a shame that this all occurred on a Saturday morning – we could have done with extra bodies. Still, I will make absolutely sure that those who are here get through this safely and in one piece."

"I know you will, Mr Randall. I can see God's strength guiding you and I have every faith that your determination will see us through."

God's strength? What are you talking about, you senile old bat? There's no God here. You're better off putting your faith in me.

Randall grinned. "Well, I am glad to have the support of a fine woman such as yourself. If you'll excuse me for a moment."

Shirley left him alone. He moved off into the corner of the room, and from inside his pocket he pulled out his Blackberry phone.

There were no emails or messages.

He cursed under his breath. If he didn't get in touch with the outside world soon he was going to blow a fuse. He needed to know what was being done to rectify this situation, but there was nothing coming through, and his attempts to call out had failed. He'd also tried several of the computers in the various offices, but none of them had an active Internet connection any longer. Communications were well and truly down it seemed.

But he still had to keep trying. The more he knew, the better he could take charge of the situation. Like they say, knowledge is power.

Randall switched off his phone to save the battery then put it away. He turned around and approached Victor who was inventorying their supplies. "How are things looking?"

Victor folded his arms and shrugged. "Not too bad. We're good for water, but don't have much food besides the odds-and-ends we found in the offices. All of the snack machines are downstairs."

"Perhaps Joe and Grace will find something in the warehouse. Didn't Mason say there are cafeteria supplies there?"

Victor nodded. "Mason just left for the warehouse to go and help them find their way around. They should all be back soon."

"Okay. If they manage to find any food, I want you in charge of it. We need to ration."

Victor grinned. "Would be my pleasure. Do you not think everyone will share?"

"No I don't. If it's one thing I know about people, it's that they are incapable of governing themselves."

"Fair enough. You can leave things safe with me."

Randall left the Scotsman alone with the inventory and approached the next person in the room, who happened to be Cosby – or Bill if he were to use the man's actual name. The aging Black man was busy piling up makeshift weaponry on a table.

Randall looked over the collected items. "Don't happen to have a shotgun hidden there, do you?"

"I wish. All I could find was stationary. There're some metal metre-rulers which could break a few bones, but not against anything big. A blade from a paper guillotine was probably the most lethal thing I could find, although it's a bit clumsy. There was this in one of the labs, though." He held up a large container full of clear liquid. "Sulphuric acid. If I remember high school chemistry well enough then I think this stuff is pretty lethal."

"It certainly is. In fact, Black Remedy owns a manufacturer that produces chemicals just like this. I've seen what this stuff can do. I'm sure it will come in handy."

Bill went back to what he was doing and Randall exited the room, closing the door behind him. The corridor was empty, other than the large stack of office furniture piled up at one end.

Two doors down was a room marked: TODD SPETCHLEY, HEAD OF PRIMATE CARE. Randall entered the room and stepped inside. The space was mostly empty, its furniture removed for the barricade. Some things still remained, however: a desk – too vast to remove – and a steel filing cabinet that was fastened to the rear wall by several bolts. Randall took a key from his pocket and unlocked the cabinet.

He'd found the key earlier while everybody was busy, still in its lock, and he had looked inside the cabinet it belonged to. Inside he had discovered several bags of crisps and a chocolate bar, amongst the useless paperwork and files. He had cleared out the cabinet earlier and replaced the contents with supplies. It now contained several bottles of water and some additional snacks that he had found in various drawers and cupboards. There was also a scalpel from the laboratory – just in case he needed to defend himself. There were many other things inside, but not everything in the cupboard had an obvious use just yet. The way he saw it was that the more he had available, the more options he would have later.

After switching off the battery, Randall placed his Blackberry inside the cupboard. It wouldn't do to be caught with it on his person after he had declined to declare it. He would return to it later and try to gain contact with somebody outside of the zoo. Somebody had to be doing something, and if there was, he would be the hero to arrange for rescue.

After locking the cabinet up again and pocketing the key, Randall re-entered the corridor and immediately bumped into Joe's group. He hoped that they were not suspicious.

"Hello everyone," he said as inconspicuously as he could. "How did it go in the warehouse?"

Mason was smiling. "Very well, as it happens. Fortunately, a delivery for the cafeteria came in this very morning, right before things became...inconvenient. There is enough food to last us for a while."

The little boy, Danny, spoke up next. "We found weapons, too, and an alligator!"

Randall raised an eyebrow. "Really?"

"Yeah," said the boy's father. "We found the litter spikes and Mason found us some gardening equipment when he came down to help; shovels, pitchforks, and some other stuff. As for the alligator, it's all dealt with. We managed to kill it. It got in through an open side-door in the warehouse, but we closed it up and blocked it."

"Excellent. I'm just glad you're all okay. Perhaps when this is all done, you can get on one of those shows where they wrestle alligators for entertainment." Randall laughed, pleased with hi banter. "Victor and the rest of us managed to secure the floor quite well so it looks like we're in good shape. It's getting dark outside so it may be a good time to bed down soon. I'm sure the shock is liable to be getting to everyone by now."

"Do we have any blankets?" Grace asked.

Randall shook his head. "There're a few cushions and some lab coats to lie on, but other than that we're in for an uncomfortable night in the cold."

Joe shrugged. "We'll manage. Things could be worse."

The lights cut out.

"You're kidding me."

CHAPTER 13

THE HUMANS FESTERED inside like rotting ants. He would rip them to pieces soon and they would scream his name in terror. Nero, they would scream. Nero. And then he would shed the name they placed upon him and become the king nature had always intended him to be. Creatures of all kinds were looking for him to lead them – and lead them he would.

* * *

The entire group helped bring food up from the warehouse, leaving about a third behind in case something happened to the main supply. They had filled up the seminar room with goods and were now piling cushions onto the floor. It was almost full dark outside and no stars were shining. They didn't have much time left until all visibility was extinguished.

Joe threw the last cushion onto his pile and put Danny down on top of it. His son's eyelids were already half-closed by the time his head hit the soft fabric. Today was too much for a child to have to deal with, and the large portion of found chocolate cake Danny had wolfed down earlier had only added to his sleepiness.

"Sweet dreams, son," said Joe, covering his son with a spare lab coat. "Tomorrow will be better."

Danny muttered, "Night, Dad," then was fast asleep. Joe sat and watched him for a while. He was such a small boy, but so brave – full of energy and optimism. Joe hadn't spent enough time with Danny since the divorce and it upset him to realise how little he knew about his son's inner-strength.

Grace came and sat down beside the two of them. "What do you think happened to the electricity?"

Joe shrugged. "I don't know, but it can't be good. Things must be really bad for the grid to be down."

"I guess so. Mason told me the zoo has a backup generator, but it only runs to the indoor exhibits – the lizards and stuff. We're going to be freezing tonight."

"Doesn't look like we'll get any breaks, does it?"

"I don't know about that. We were lucky with the cafeteria delivery. Least we won't starve. You should have a sandwich; everyone else has."

Joe nodded. "Maybe later. I guess we can hole up here for a while. It's not too cold at the moment either. Least we're not having a load of snow like we did year. I thought that was the final winter to end all winters. We'll get through this."

Grace looked him in the eye and seemed serious all of a sudden. "We're lucky to have you, Joe. You saved my life today. Bill's too. We owe you our lives."

"You don't owe me anything. I just did what anyone would have."

Grace frowned. "You think? I can't see Shirley risking herself like you did."

"Okay, I did what most people would have done."

Grace moved closer and lay against him. Her skin felt warm. "You did what only brave people would have done. I'm really glad you're here. Danny too."

Joe felt awkward for a moment. He hadn't had a woman this close to him in years and it made him nervous, but at the same time very relaxed. "I'm glad you're here too, Grace," he finally admitted, wrapping an arm around her. "I don't think I could have looked after Danny today without you."

Grace looked up at him. "He's a great kid."

"You should thank his mother for that. I haven't been around so much lately."

Joe expected Grace to investigate further, but she didn't. "You're making up for it now," was all she said.

"Thanks," said Joe, disagreeing with the comment but grateful that she had said it. Whether or not she heard his gratitude, he did not know. Grace was already asleep.

It wasn't particularly late, but Joe guessed it had been a long day for everyone. The others in the group had also begun to settle down into their own little areas. Bill and Mason were close by, while Randall, Shirley, and Victor sat further back in the room. Victor had built his bed beneath one of the study-desks. For what reason, Joe did not know.

It was now fully dark outside and Joe could see the night between the gaps in the barricade that Victor had assembled in front of the window. He wondered what the evening would bring. Would the animals sleep? Or would they become even more active? Did they even need to sleep? Whatever had affected the creatures seemed to have taken complete control of them.

As if to answer his questions, creatures outside began to howl, using whatever particular vocal abilities they had. At the far end of the room Randall got up from his pillow-bed and went to the window.

"What's happening?" Bill asked him.

"I don't know," Randall replied. "I can't really see anything. They're out there, though. I can hear them."

"They know we're in here," said Victor. "They want our blood."

"That may well be," said Randall, "but we're safe in here. There's no reason to worry."

But as the volume of the catcalls increased, Joe couldn't help but do just that. It was several hours before he got to sleep.

CHAPTER 14

I T WAS PITCH black when Joe awoke. He had no idea what time it was, and for a few moments forgot where he was. The darkness extinguished his vision and made remembering hard, but when his ears tuned in to the animal noises outside, it all came rushing back.

Everything's gone to shit. The animals...

That wasn't what had woken him though. There was somebody walking about. Joe strained his eyes, trying to see through the darkness. He could make out nothing solid, but someone was definitely there, creeping around in the shadows.

Should I shout out?

No, I'll keep quiet. I have no reason to think they're up to anything.

Joe felt around himself, checking for Danny and Grace. They were both close by, sleeping soundly and breathing rhythmically. He was also pretty sure he could make out Bill's silhouette nearby too. The sneaking person would have to have been Mason, Randall, Victor, or Shirley. With the exception of Mason, Joe didn't trust any of them. Again, he considered calling out, but still chose to remain quiet.

Probably just someone going to the toilets down the hallway.

After the mystery person left the room, Joe waited ten more minutes before he could take it no longer. Sleep would be impossible unless he knew where everyone was. He got up slowly, so that he wouldn't wake the others, and crept to the door in the same way that the mystery person had; an almost impossible feat in the pitch black dark. He kept his arms out as feelers to keep from bumping into the walls.

Outside in the corridor it was no easier to see, the dark was just as suffocating. The air was cooler, though, and tasted fresher than the recycled atmosphere of the seminar room. Joe took a deep breath and looked left and right whilst cocking his ear to one side. It wasn't clear where the other person had gone but, as Joe listened, he thought he could detect sounds coming from further down the corridor.

Moist, slapping sounds.

Joe realised the animals inside the lab were no longer making noise – the first time since Mason had riled them up by chancing upon them. Joe felt a tightening in his chest. The smart thing to do would be to wake the others, but something urged him to go on alone. If he was going to alert everyone, he at least wanted sufficient reason. They had all been through enough.

Taking one tentative step after the other, Joe approached the lab, listening intently and trying to identify the slapping sounds. The noises seemed louder as he stood outside the door to the lab. He reached for the handle.

Someone grabbed him from behind.

Joe spun around. His heart threatened to leap out of his throat. Whoever had grabbed him was invisible in the darkness, only the dim shape of them visible.

"Whoa there, Joe! It's Bill. Didn't mean to scare you."

Joe couldn't speak. He sucked in giant gulps of air. It was several moments before he managed to catch his breath enough to say anything. "Christ almighty. You sneak up and grab me in the dark and you didn't mean to scare me?"

"Guess you have a point there, sorry. You're the one wondering around in the night, though. What are you up to?"

Joe's eyes adjusted to the dark sufficiently that he could make out Bill's curious expression. "Actually, I'm not the one wondering around. There's someone in the lab. I was about to find out who."

"Okay," said Bill, a hint of concern in his voice. "Lead the way."

Joe nodded but was unsure if the other man could see it in the dark. He turned back around and wrapped his fingers around the door handle agaun.

Here goes.

He opened the door.

Inside, the lab was an unending blanket of darkness, except for a floating torchlight at the far end. Joe could not make out who was holding it.

"Who is it?" Bill whispered.

"I don't know. I can't see anything in here."

"Light the burners," Bill suggested.

"What do you mean?"

Bill placed a hand on Joe's shoulder to find him in the dark. "The Bunson Burners run on gas. We could still light them even with no electricity."

Joe thought about it. "Good idea. You got a lighter?"

Bill didn't say anything but in the dark Joe felt the other man hand him a small metallic object. A flip lighter. Joe sparked it up and the flame lit a narrow cone of light around him, enough to navigate his way carefully over to one of the lab benches.

A few sweeps with the lighter and Joe managed to locate a row of gas taps. He released the valve on the first, waited for the hiss, lit it, and adjusted the flame to its highest. It took only a few seconds to light several more, but it still did not allow Joe to see who was flittering about at the other end of the lab. The light of the burners stretched only a few feet from the centre of the room.

Nothing left to do but shout out. So that's what Joe did. "Who's there?"

The torch beam spun erratically as the person realised they were not alone, the tunnel of light eventually finding its way into Joe's face and blinding him. Bill came up beside him and stood shoulder to shoulder.

"We said who's there?" Bill's voice was strong and forceful, much tougher than Joe's. "Show yourself now, or else."

The torchlight bobbed about as the person approached them. Joe thought for a moment that it felt like being in a train's headlights. His eyes were forced shut as the torch continued to shine in his face. His retinas ached.

"How ya doing there, pals? Up to some late night dogging?"

Joe frowned at the Scottish accent, knowing who it belonged to: Victor.

"You really don't know anything about gay people, do you?" Bill said.

Victor laughed. "Less I know the better, pal."

"We're not up to anything," Joe stated. "We're here to see what you're up to."

"No problem," said Victor. "Best you see for yourself."

The torchlight left Joe's face and circled the room, illuminating the rows and rows of cages on each wall. The animals inside were no longer making a fuss. In fact a lot of the cages were now open.

Joe's eyes went wide. "Shit, you let them all out!"

Victor laughed, the sound echoing through the unlit room. He stepped forward into the light of the Bunson Burners and Joe saw that he was drenched in blood from head to toe. His tattoos were merged with gore and a dead bird hung limply from his left hand. Martha glinted in his right.

Victor's laughing continued. He held the gutted animal up like a trophy. "Aye, I let them all out, I did, but only long enough to slit their throats."

Joe stared at the blood-soaked knife in Victor's hand and had to swallow back a mouthful of vomit. "You're insane."

"No, pal. Just practical. Now do me a favour and leave a man to his work. We can all use this meat if things get bad enough."

"Things are already that bad," said Bill, grabbing Joe's arm and pulling him backwards. "Come on, Joe."

Together, they backed away from Victor, not taking their eyes off of him – or his beloved Martha – until they reached the door. Joe's back hit the wood and he flinched, spun around. He snatched at the door handle, missing several times, but finally getting a grip and flinging it open. He and Bill barrelled through into the corridor outside like Hell itself was behind them.

"That guy is batshit crazy," said Bill, huffing and puffing as the two of them hurried down the unlit hallway. "He even killed the birds, and they weren't even dangerous. I think he enjoys it,"

"I know," Joe agreed. "We need to warn the others."

They reached the seminar room and Joe shoved open the door. Everyone inside woke with a start, shouting out garbled utterances as they were yanked away from their dreams. Joe closed the door and leant his back up against it. "Everyone wake up."

"We're already awake! What's going on? Are we under attack?" Joe recognised the startled voice as belonging to Grace.

"Yes, would you care to explain?" said another voice that could only have been Randall's.

The room lit up. Joe saw that Bill had managed to rustle up some torches from the stockpile and was placing them around the room to light up as big an area as possible. Joe could now make out the concerned faces of the others in the room. Fortunately, Danny was still asleep.

My son could sleep through the end of the world. Lucky for him, because that may just be what's happening.

"Victor's gone mad!" Joe blurted it out, unsure of any other way to approach the subject.

Randall stood up and moved to the centre of the room. "What on Earth are you talking about?"

"He's in the lab, right now" said Bill. "Hacking away at all the animals in their cages. They're all dead."

"That's good isn't it?" Shirley asked. "They were a danger."

Mason was shaking his head, a hand against his brow. "No, no, no. We agreed that they were to be left alone."

"That's beside the point," said Joe. "What matters is that Victor is going around killing things like a twisted maniac."

"Of course he is," said Randall. "That's exactly what I advised him to do."

Both of Joe's eyelids opened wide. "I'm sorry, what?"

"I said I told him to do it. The animals in those cages were dangerous. How could we rest with an enemy within our boundaries? Plus, the meat they provide may prove invaluable in the days ahead."

Mason sighed. "They were invaluable until Victor killed them all."

"I stand by what I said. We are in too much trouble to risk those things getting out. I voiced my concerns to Shirley and Victor, and Victor was happy to oblige. The man is doing us all a service."

"I agree," said Shirley. "Those beasts would happily have done the same to us."

Joe shook his head. What could he say? There was a certain amount of logic to their argument and, if he was honest, it did feel safer knowing that the caged animals were no longer a concern. It didn't make him feel any better about Victor, though. The image of the Scotsman dripping with blood and shrouded in shadow was permanently etched into his brain. Regardless of what anybody said, Victor was dangerous.

Joe just didn't know how dangerous yet.

CHAPTER 15

THE MORNING ARRIVED in silence. No birds sang their morning tunes and no cars hummed along distant motorways. The world was still.

Randall had been awake for five minutes, but had done nothing except observe the others sleeping. The incident during the night had riled everyone up, but they had eventually gotten back to sleep. Victor had not returned, most likely still gutting the animals in the lab, collecting their meat. Randall found out that Victor was a Scot's Guard as a younger man and more than capable of doing the tasks that others were not. Whether the group agreed or not, Victor should be commended for his pragmatism, not derided.

It had been enjoyable to watch Joe and Mason back down and accept that harsh methods were needed, not fluffy thinking. They needed to understand that normal rules no longer applied. Randall was going to teach them all that lesson one way or the other.

The room began to glow as cold grey shafts of dawn-light crept in through the gaps in the window's barricade. The others in the room began to stir. Randall noticed that there was one other person, besides Victor, who was missing. Grace wasn't there.

Where have you gotten to, my pretty? This is no time for a woman to be walking around unescorted.

Randall pushed himself up off the floor. His joints cracked, his fifty-year-old body unhappy at spending the night on a thin pile of cushions. It wasn't something he was sure he could ever get used to, but for now there was no other choice. He stretched out his arms, listened to his elbows click one last time, and ambled over to the seminar room's exit. Thankfully no one woke and he was free to go about his business undisturbed. He intended to find Grace and see what the woman was doing, but first he had other things to attend to. Randall was satisfied that the corridor outside was empty of both people and, more importantly, animals, so he stepped outside.

He approached the Head of Primates office across the hall and opened the door quietly. Once inside, he closed it just as carefully behind him. The key to the room's filing cabinet was in his pocket and he plucked it out, using it on the lock a moment later. He took a packet of biscuits from the middle-shelf and popped one into his mouth.

Breakfast.

Once he'd finished several more biscuits, Randall placed the packet back inside the cupboard and grabbed the next item on the shelf – his Blackberry. He pressed the 'ON' button and waited for the phone to boot up. It took several minutes, but when it finally activated, something unexpected occurred.

< ONE NEW MESSAGE >

Randall thumbed at the keypad clumsily, failing several times to get the message up, but eventually succeeding. He could not believe what it said:

RE: Emergency Communication

This is a Government message to all cellular devices. Emergency Rescue Operations are on-going at the following locations: Aberdeen, Bristol, Barnham, Blackpool, Dudley, Leicester, Ipswich, Nottingham, Oxford, Preston, Salford, Torquay, Taunton, Warwick, Winchester, Yeovil. If you are able to, please head to these areas. Help will be forthcoming. Do not approach any animal.

Randall stared at his phone for several minutes, re-reading the message over and over. Despite his misgivings, the Government was indeed addressing the situation and were possibly even gaining a foothold. Or are they? Randall considered that the message could have been sent automatically by a dusty computer in the Home Office, and that the areas mentioned were already overrun by animal attacks. The message did not guarantee that help was available. They were probably still safer staying put. Some of the locations were nearby – Leicester especially – and it was perhaps an option to try and reach them. He would have to think about things before making a decision.

Randall switched off the Blackberry and placed it back inside the cabinet. He locked it up and pocketed the key. Then he left.

Outside, in the hallway, he bumped unexpectedly into Victor. The man had cleaned himself up and was now wearing a baggy, brown jump suit that looked as though it belonged to the zoo's maintenance staff.

Randall raised an eyebrow. "New outfit?"

"Aye, I found it in the warehouse. My other clothes were a wee bit...sticky."

"Indeed. What are you up to now?"

"Just checking the building's security, making sure none of the furry bastards can get in."

Randall patted the man on his shoulder and moved past. "Keep up the good work."

As he walked back down the corridor, Victor shouted after him. "And what exactly have you been up to, pal?"

Randall stopped and turned around. He thought about the message on his phone before answering. "Me? Nothing, Victor. Nothing at all."

The less you know the better, my friend. Until I decide otherwise.

Victor scrutinised Randall for a few minutes and eventually cracked a crooked-tooth smile. "Well, let me know if you need help with whatever it is that you're not doing. I'm very good with secrets."

Victor sauntered off, leaving Randall alone to consider his comments.

CHAPTER 16

JOE AWOKE TO screaming. He it was Grace as soon as he saw she was missing from her bed.

Danny woke up. "What's happening, Dad?"

"I don't know. Stay here while I find out."

Danny looked worried, but nodded. Joe patted him on the shoulders, kissed his forehead. He then scrambled over to Bill. "Bill, watch Danny while I go find out what's going on. I think it's Grace."

"Of course, go!"

Joe entered the corridor, wanting to rush but trying not to until he knew the situation better. Another scream sounded and he couldn't help but pick up speed.

The noise continued, coming from one of the offices on his right. Joe pinpointed it to a room marked JEFFREY CARLSON, HEAD VET. He opened the door and pushed himself inside. Grace stood in the middle of the room, shrieking, and clutching at her face. Joe examined the floor in front of her and saw the reason why.

"What the hell?"

She flinched at the sound of Joe's voice and looked over at him. Her eyes were unnaturally wide. "What do I do?" she asked.

Joe peered down at the creatures by her feet – massive, hairy spiders and armour-plated scorpions. The zoo's entire creepy crawly menagerie was surrounding Grace in a tightening semi-circle of hissing, spitting menace.

Joe stretched his arms out towards her. "Grace, very slowly...come here."

Grace shook her head. "I can't. They'll get me."

As if to agree with her, several tarantulas rose up on their hind legs and hissed. A cloud of bristly, brown hairs filled the air around them. Grace let out another scream.

"You have to move now, Grace! They're getting closer."

Grace stopped her screaming and attempted to get herself under control, almost hyperventilating in the process. Joe held his breath, waiting for her to do something. It was a relief when she finally managed to take a step backwards.

"That's it. Really slowly."

Grace took another step but one of the tarantulas scuttled around and blocked her path. It stood between her and Joe.

How the hell did it know to do that? Spiders can't behave like this, can they?

"Stay still, Grace. I need to think a second."

The creatures moved closer. She shrieked again, but managed to get it under control before it took hold. Joe glanced around the room for something to help, but it was just an ordinary office and most the furniture had been taken out. There was nothing he could use.

So he did the only thing he could think of.

Joe lifted his size-eleven trainer and brought it down on top of the tarantula. It hissed and squirmed beneath his heel, but he kept the pressure on, feeling its spindly legs snapping with each twist of his ankle. He lifted his foot again and expected to see a sickly mush, but it was just the same spider – crumpled and broken, but the same.

"Grace, come on!"

Grace saw the opportunity and found enough courage to make a run for it. She took several lunging steps towards him and threw herself into his arms. For a few moments, Joe just held her, glad that she was safe. Then he realised they weren't out of the woods yet. "We need to get out of here," he said, grabbing Grace by the arm. She winced and Joe saw why. "Hey, what happened to your wrist?"

Grace eyed the thick gash on the back of her forearm, then looked down at the army of approaching arachnids. "Now's not the time."

Joe leapt to the door and held it open. Grace ran through it, followed by a scuttling army of thrashing scorpions and spiders.

Joe slammed the door shut, catching an obsidian scorpion against the frame and crushing it to a viscous pulp. "Are you...okay?" he asked Grace between panting breaths.

Grace nodded, but tears had released themselves and were gliding down her cheeks. "I'm fine."

"So, are you going to tell me what happened?"

Grace stared at the floor. "I....I woke up and I was cold, so I was looking for some blankets. Those things just came out of nowhere. I still don't know how they got inside."

"But how did you hurt your arm? It looks really bad."

Grace held up the puckered wound and examined it. Blood was still coursing from the cut, but had started to slow down. "I don't know," she said. "Maybe one of those things got me."

Joe wasn't buying it. Something about the way she wouldn't look him in the eye told him that other things were going on. He shook his head. "They wouldn't be able to do that type of damage. That's a cut not a bite."

Grace's eyes narrowed. "I don't know then. Does it matter?"

"It does to me, but let's just get it patched up for now."

Grace tensed up, the features of her face contorting under a sudden rigor. "You okay?"

Grace stopped breathing, bent over and slumped against the wall. Her leg shot out to the side. Joe looked down and saw something moving.

A bright yellow scorpion was deeply embedded in Grace's calf by its stinger. She screamed.

Joe reached down and grabbed the vile creature. The feel of its brittle exoskeleton was repulsive as he flung it against the wall. It shattered upon impact.

But what damage has it done already?

Joe turned to Grace.

Just in time to catch her fall.

CHAPTER 17

JOE RUSHED INTO the seminar room with an unconscious Grace in his arms. He prayed that it was shock and not some sort of toxin from the scorpion.

Mason leapt up from behind one of the desks. "What's happened?"

Joe lay Grace down on top of the nearest table. "She got bitten by a scorpion."

Mason went pale, all colour flushing from his cheeks. "What did it look like?"

"I don't know. It was small and yellow."

Mason held his head in his hands before staring hard at Joe. "Leiurus quinquestriatus."

"In English?"

"Deathstalker Scorpion, also known as the Israeli Desert Scorpion. Its venom is amongst the worst of all species."

"Why the hell would you have those things around?" asked Bill, rushing over to help.

Mason shrugged. He looked so tired that even such a simple movement seemed like an ordeal. "They were kept in the World of Venom building. How they got over here, I don't know."

"They've gotten smart," said Joe. "There were spiders and scorpions in one of the offices. They attacked Grace in a group, working together."

"This is not good. Arachnida have been affected."

Joe rubbed Grace's forehead and brushed her damp hair out of her face. "Let's worry about that later. We need to help her."

"There's little that we can do," Mason explained. "Get some soap and clean the wound, then elevate her leg. With rest, she should hopefully be okay. There's adrenaline in the lab if she has an allergic reaction, but that doesn't seem to be the case fortunately."

"Why did she pass out then?"

"Shock perhaps. Maybe it's blood-loss from that cut on her arm. How did she get that?"

"I don't know. She wouldn't tell me." Joe examined the gash on Grace's arm. It had started to dry, but the surrounding area was caked in dark brown blood. It needed stitches.

Danny came up and held Joe's hand. "Is Grace going to be okay, Dad?"

"She's fine, Danny. Will be much better after a sleep."

"You promise?"

"Of course. You remember when Macho Man got bitten by Jake the Snake's python, don't you? He got better."

Danny smiled up at him. "Okay."

Bill returned with a bottle of hand soap and started rubbing it on Grace's bite. The flesh was red and swollen. Joe gathered some cushions and piled them beneath her ankle. She was still unconscious, but seemed peaceful, as though trapped in a gentle dream.

"I'm sure she'll be fine," said Bill.

"I hope so." Joe looked around the room and saw that both Victor and Randall were missing. Shirley was still napping at the back of the room, obviously uninterested in recent events. "Where are Randall and Victor?"

Bill shrugged.

"I'm here and Victor is in the hallway," said Randall, entering the room. "Is that alright with you?"

Joe turned around. "Fine. Just like to know that everyone is safe and accounted for."

Mason stepped in front of Joe and addressed Randall. "And what is Victor doing in the hallway exactly? Looking for more endangered animals to hack to pieces?"

"We already discussed that, Mr Mason. It was agreed that Victor's actions were in the best interests of the group."

Mason took offence to the man's statement and told him so. "Actually it was not agreed, Mr Randall. It was a decision that you seemed to make all on your own."

"Yeah," Bill added. "What gives you the right to make decisions for the rest of us?"

Randall placed his palms together in front of himself as if to implore their mercy. "Now let's be reasonable, my friends. In the current circumstances things need to happen with a certain amount of...urgency. There is not always time to consult one another and hold a team meeting. Shirley, Victor, and I did what we thought was best. If it wasn't a popular decision then I apologise, but it has happened now so let's move on."

Joe sighed. "Just don't make decisions behind our backs again, okay?"

Randall rolled his eyes, but nodded in agreement. A moment later, he seemed to finally notice that Grace was lying unconscious on the table. He raised a coarse black eyebrow at the others curiously.

"A scorpion bit her," Joe explained. "Hopefully she'll sleep it off."

"A scorpion? Things keep getting better and better. I assume the danger has been dealt with?"

"Dealt with, as in the room they were in is locked up and secure."

Randall sighed. "Another room that's off limits? We'll have nowhere left soon."

"Joe said the scorpions were working as a team," said Bill.

"I guess we can safely assume that is true," Randall agreed, "but how on earth did scorpions get on the second floor?"

Joe shrugged. "I really have no idea, but if they keep staging attacks we'll end up trapped and cornered before long."

Randall walked over to the room's window and looked out through one of the gaps in the barricade. "Then we need to hit back. I think it's time that we attack them."

"How?" asked Joe. "What the hell can we do?"

Randall turned away from the window and faced the room like some pudgy statesman. "I don't know yet, but I'm guessing there's someone that may have a few ideas."

Joe folded his arms. "Victor?"

Bill huffed air through his nostrils. "That guy's a psychopath, but I hate to admit that might be a good thing right now."

"Didn't expect to see you on that man's side," said Joe.

"I'm not, but if he enjoys killing animals as much as he seems to then he's probably our biggest asset right now."

"Aye, that I am, pal. That I am."

Joe rolled his eyes. "You can't mention anyone around here without them suddenly popping up from somewhere."

"Then perhaps you shouldn't talk behind people's backs, pal."

"That's not what we were doing."

"No? Did I not hear the word psychopath being bandied about?" Victor glared at Bill who seemed to shrink away. "Don't worry yourselves. I've been called worse."

"So, Victor," said Randall, "if you heard our conversation, then perhaps you might have some advice for us."

"You mean about your little counter-strike? Aye, I could think of a thing or two. We need to get that big bastard ape. He's their general."

"Really," said Joe. "You think they have a leader?"

"Aye. You've all seen the way he hangs back while others attack us in groups. He's been sending in wave after wave. First, the infantry downstairs – the monkeys – and then the bloody SAS lemurs that came through the windows."

"And the scorpions that got Grace," added Bill.

Victor nodded and looked at Grace, unconscious on the table. "We're at war people. Under siege. The only way we can end it is to take the heart out of their army." He looked around the room, making eye contact with each of them. "We have to kill that bloody silverback."

CHAPTER 18

IT WAS EXCITING, teasing and toying with the humans. The first few attacks so far had succeed only in spreading fear – but that was the point. While he could storm their tower right now and tear them all to pieces, Nero wanted the human's to experience the feeling of being trapped – caged. Like all of the animals in this zoo, the human's would know what it was to be completely at the mercy of a heartless master. It was too much fun to let this end too quickly, but eventually he would become bored. Then Nero would strike his final blow and seek out more humans to extinguish. Very soon it would be mankind that was endangered.

* * *

It was almost dark again, Joe noticed. They had been making preparations all day, thinking up ways to strike back at the animals. They had collected anything that could be thrown as a projectile: paperweights, PC monitors, text books (after persuading Mason that they were necessary for the sacrifice), and other assorted junk. Victor had also filled some glass beakers with the sulphuric acid from the lab and then wrapped them up in paper towels. A canister of petrol that Bill had brought up from the warehouse would also allow them to set light to toilet rolls (of which they had many) and hurl them from the windows. It wasn't much, but hopefully it would show that they intended to put up a fight.

Everybody carried a weapon. After what had happened to Grace it was clear that an attack could come at any time. Joe held one of the litter pickers in his hand as he went up to check on Grace. She had recently awoken but was not yet fully coherent, drifting in and out of lucidity for the last few hours.

"Grace, are you awake?"

Her eyelids fluttered. "J-Joe?"

"Yeah, it's me. How you feeling?"

"Like," she swallowed – the sound was dry and rasping. "I got stung by a scorpion."

Joe laughed. "That must be the fever talking. Scorpions attacking people is insane."

Grace smiled weakly. "How is Danny?"

"Don't worry about anyone else. We're all fine. You should try and go back to sleep."

Grace nodded and rolled onto her side. As she did so she pulled her arm up against her waist. Joe noticed her deep wound again. It was healing well but he still wanted to know what had caused it.

"Grace? Will you tell me how you hurt your arm?"

She breathed heavily and Joe thought she may have already fallen asleep, but then she spoke softly. "I need my pills."

"Pills? What pills? Grace?"

She was gone, pulled into a fevered slumber that could not be disturbed. Joe thought about what she had meant.

Pills? What pills does she need?

"How she doing?" Bill asked.

"She's a bit out of it, but I think she's okay. At least I hope so."

"I don't think scorpion stings are lethal."

Joe nodded and took a seat on some cushions beside Bill on the floor. He folded his long legs underneath him. "Mason said the same. Doesn't mean it does you any good."

"She'll be fine. Don't worry."

Joe sighed. "To be honest, it's not the scorpion bite that worries me."

"Oh? Then what?"

"She has a horrible cut on her arm and she won't explain how she got it. In fact the last time I asked she just told me that she 'needed her pills'."

"Her pills?"

"Yeah. What you think she meant?"

"Painkillers perhaps? Who knows, but it's probably nothing. We can find out as soon as she's herself again."

Joe lay back against the cushions and stretched out his legs. "I suppose so." He decided to change the subject; thinking about Grace just upset him. "You think we can actually fight back tomorrow?"

Bill shrugged. "Bunch of farm animals and monkeys? How hard can it be?"

"Something tells me it's not going to be so easy. I don't know what's happened to them all, but I don't think they're normal anymore. They're smarter. Maybe a virus has affected their brains or something?"

"They're demons." Shirley walked over and sat in front of Bill and Joe. "Sent to put an end to our sin."

Bill sighed. "Again with the sin? What are you harping on about now, woman?"

Shirley seemed oblivious to the comment and carried on her ranting. "I once met an Irishman who told me all about the Lord. He told me that God's patience is thin and that all of us are on the cusp of his vengeance."

"And what does that mean?" Joe asked.

"It means that enough is enough. All the fucking and fighting in this world has to stop and He has ways of making us realise that."

"Ways?"

"Yes! The Irishman told me that God can destroy us on a whim. He flooded the earth once and now he is completing what he began back then."

Bill laughed. "You're talking about Noah and his ark?"

"No, I am talking about what is happening now. We're being wiped out. By God and his vengeance. Our sin has become too much for Him to tolerate any longer. He has unleashed a plague of beasts upon the Earth."

Joe wanted to argue. The woman was so full of bile that it would be nice to shut her up. For some reason, though, he couldn't find the words to disagree. God was as good a reason as any for all of this. Joe did have a question however: "Who was this Irishman that knew so much. Did he have a name?"

Shirley looked at Joe and seemed to hear something other than her own voice for the first time. "Not one that he gave me. He was a traveller. At first I thought he was just a drunken rogue, but he knew things – intimate things – about me. Things no one could ever know. He told me that once he was an angel, but that he now lived amongst humans. I learned about Heaven and Hell from this man. He showed me the light."

"And why did this ex-angel..." Joe put a hand to his head and chuckled. "I can't believe these words are coming out of my mouth: why did this ex-angel decide to share all of this knowledge with you?"

"Because he needed beer money."

Bill and Joe spluttered and laughed in unison. Joe had to stifle himself to keep from waking up Danny. "Beer money? Okay, Shirley, wherever you're keeping the wacky-backy, let us in on it."

Shirley's face contorted into craggy lines of anger. "Fools," she spat. "If you choose not to heed my warnings then on your head be it."

"What warnings?" Bill asked. "All you've done is spout fairy tales."

"My warning is this: get your affairs in order, people, because we'll all be in Hell soon – and some of us deserve worse fates than others."

Shirley stomped away and Joe shook his head in disbelief. "That woman is a Grade A wacko!"

"Tell me about it," said Bill. "You think she was delusional before everything happened, or if it was this shit that made her lose it?"

"She was probably already losing the cheese off her cracker and this just helped her along her way."

"Still, makes you wonder if any of what she said is true."

Joe frowned at Bill. "You mean about God punishing us all and that we're all going to Hell? No, I don't believe it. It's insane."

"It is insane, but then so is all of the animals turning on us."

"You're right," said Joe. "Maybe we are all going to Hell."

"Or perhaps we're already there," said Bill.

CHAPTER 19

I T WAS ALMOST time, Randall decided. The sun was rising and it would not be long before there was daylight. Everyone else was still asleep but Randall was wide awake and staring out of the seminar room window, surveying what would soon become his battlefield. The orange light of dawn cast over everything and gave the landscape an ethereal glow, like some consecrated ground due to be made holy. To be blessed with the sacred blood of battle.

Victor, no doubt, had more tactical knowledge than anybody else, but the man was not a leader. Randall would be the one to organise and lead the group. Under his order they would prosper. He would enable them to regain some semblance of order from this suddenly mad world – and then they would thank him for it.

Legends are forged in the fires of battle.

Randall looked outside at the enemy's army. It had grown overnight to contain an all manner of species, many of which he still could not name, despite his recent research. He theorised that the animals which escaped first had set about freeing the others, liberating the entire zoo in some sort of prisoner of war escapade. Randall estimated at least five hundred animals were now amassed outside the building – and standing amidst them all was a towering giant: the silverback.

My counterpart. The Napoleon to my Nelson.

Randall went over to a collection of nearby desks. Victor had stacked them full of projectiles in order of priority. The gas bombs were to be used first to create disarray in the ranks and to force the animals into another attack. Then the PC monitors and other assorted heavy objects would be used as ballast to deter any animals that tried to scale the building's walls. Acid bombs would be used to attack anything that managed to get through the windows. After that, it would be hand to hand combat.

Hopefully it won't reach a skirmish. We don't have the numbers for it.

Randall turned around and saw that Victor was awake, lying beneath a table and staring at him.

"Morning, Victor."

Victor smirked. "Seems like I catch you wandering around on your own quite a lot, pal."

"I just like to keep on top of things. Someone has to."

"Aye, and that someone is you, is it?"

Randall lifted his head high, eyeballs pointed downwards. "Unless there's someone else that wants the job."

Victor sniffed back a nose full of phlegm and swallowed it. "Not that I can see."

"So I have your support?"

Victor remained quiet for a moment, then: "Aye, for now."

"Wonderful." Randall clapped his hands together. "Then I can rely on you to help me lead the assault."

"No way I'm gonna miss out on all the fun. We'll need to be ready soon."

"Agreed. Could you be so kind as to wake everyone in thirty minutes? We'll commence the attack in ninety. They will not take this building from us."

"Roger that." Victor started to climb out from under the table.

Randall left the other man to it. There was something he wanted to check on first. If he was about to lead an attack then he wanted all the facts at his disposal. He left the room and crossed the corridor outside, entering what he now thought of as his office – despite the name on another man's name on the door. Inside, Randall unlocked the filing cabinet and finished off the pack of biscuits he'd started on the day before.

He switched on his Blackberry.

<ONE NEW MESSAGE>

RE: Emergency Communication

This is a Government message to all cellular devices. Emergency Rescue Operations are firmly established at the following locations: Aberdeen, Bristol, Leicester, Nottingham, Torquay, Warwick. If you are able to, head to these areas. Avoid contact with all animals.

Randall studied the message and considered its meaning. Several of the earlier locations had been omitted – perhaps abandoned – but the remaining ones were now being described as 'firmly established'.

But he wasn't about to trust his future to the hands of the Government. He now had clear proof that a battle against the animals could be won. He would win today's battle and secure everyone's future at the zoo. By the time the Government rolled around, he would be the respected saviour of the group.

Randall turned off the phone and locked it back inside the cabinet. It was then that he felt the tremors.

"What was that?"

He hurried back into the corridor and re-entered the seminar room just as another tremor hit. Everyone inside the room had woken up now – with the exception of Grace who was still unconscious – and looked as confused as he was. Joe stood in front of him, holding his little boy in his gigantic arms. Randall asked what was going on.

"I don't know," said Joe. "It's like an earthquake or something."

Randall shook his head. "No. Something is hitting the building."

Victor was already at the window, pulling away some of the barricade to see through the glass. Randall moved up beside him and looked too. He could not believe what he saw.

This is not good. We've been caught napping.

"What is it?" asked Joe.

"Elephants. Elephants, Rhinos, and I think a hippopotamus."

Another tremor hit the building as an African Elephant crashed its thick torso against the building, the sound of splintering brickwork and shattering glass accompanying the impact.

"What do we do?" Joe pointed at a beetle scurrying from a widening crack in the wall.

"We do what we planned," Randall replied. "We strike back."

Victor turned from the window and started to shout. "Okay, squaddies. Get to your battle stations. Joe, you and me are up front with the fire bombs. Make sure you spread your hits to maximise bombardment area. Everyone else, get armed and ready to drop the monitors on anything that gets too close. Remember, everybody, the silverback is the priority target."

Randall stood back and watched everyone assemble. This was be his moment of glory. Years of boardroom success would not compare to this victory. This moment was going to define the rest of his life.

"Okay, everyone," Randall shouted. "Let them have it."

Joe and Victor threw the first round of firebombs.

CHAPTER 20

JOE WATCHED HIS firebomb arc through the air, flames flickering majestically in the wind. It struck a pair of snarling cheetahs and their pelts went up in a burst of heat that Joe could feel from the second floor window. In mere seconds, the flesh of the floundering big cats bubbled and blistered before sloughing off in thick sheets of spitting meat. The odour of singed fur filled the air.

Joe watched the cheetahs retreat in dying agony and turned to Victor. "It's working."

"Aye, but don't start celebrating yet, pal."

He's right, Joe thought. That was nothing but a pinprick in the ocean.

Joe picked up another firebomb, just as one of the African elephants hit the building again. The entire floor rocked and he almost dropped the volatile incendiary at his feet.

Victor shouted out so that everyone could hear. "Defend the walls!"

Bill, Shirley, and Mason rushed forward, clutching bulky PC monitors in their hands. They hoisted them through the open windows and let them go. Two of the monitors hit the elephant below, breaking into smithereens against its thick head.

It did nothing.

The elephant trumpeted in fury and then resumed its onslaught on the base of the building. The floor shook again. Plaster flakes showered from the ceiling, and Joe actually had to fight to keep his balance. "The whole building is going to come down."

"Throw another firebomb," Bill ordered.

"No," said Victor. "It's too close. We can't risk setting fire to the building."

Bill nodded and understood his error.

Joe had an idea. He went and grabbed a flask of acid from the weapons table.

I hope this works.

He headed back to the window and moved the others out of the way. "Everyone, stand back."

The elephant was still rushing the building, stepping back and then lunging at the brickwork again and again. Joe leant out of the window and held out the flask of acid. The liquid fell out as he tipped the beaker sideways. The acid doused the elephant's thick, round ears and bulbous head, but seemed to have no effect. Joe watched in anticipation as time stretched on. Just when he was certain his plan had failed, a wisp of smoke began to form. The elephant flinched, rearing up on its hind legs and thrashing its head about. It let out an agonised screech and then turned tail and fled the battlefield, trampling several smaller animals in the process.

Victor patted Joe on the back. "Good work."

Joe didn't have time to accept the compliment, the animal army outside was riled and starting to attack in force. The silverback came to the fore and beat at his chest. The ape's snarling cries sounded almost human in their fury. Joe was sure that the beast was staring him directly in the eye.

"The silverback," Victor said. "Just the bugger we want. Get yourself armed, Joe."

Joe grabbed another firebomb. Victor already had one. Together they lit the makeshift fuses and prepared to throw them.

Victor held his firebomb over his shoulder. "After three. One... two...three!"

The two men threw their firebombs in unison. They sailed through the air, both aimed at the silverback gorilla. The towering ape stared back at them, smouldering malice dripping from his eyeballs like molten hatred.

Victor's firebomb went wide and hit the ground in front of a pack of Llamas. Joe's was closer to the mark and arced right towards the silverback's face.

The gorilla swatted the projectile out of the sky.

A fireball exploded.

The silverback turned away, covering its giant head with an arm. The liquid fire crackled in the air for a few moments, releasing thick plumes of black smoke.

The silverback turned back around. One side of his face was a glistening mess of pink flesh.

Victor punched at the air. "You got the bastard."

"Barely," said Joe. "But I think he's pulling back."

Sure enough, the silverback grunted at the other animals and the whole army started turning away.

They're retreating.

Bill ran up to the window and hopped up and down. "We did it. They're going away."

Everyone in the room cheered. Danny came running up to Joe and hugged him around the waist. "You did it, Dad! You opened up a can of whoop ass on them."

"I sure did, son. I told you I wasn't going to let anyone hurt you."

Danny hugged him again then ran off to look out of the window.

"Hey, you be careful. Any of those animals start coming back and you move away from that there, you hear?"

Bill placed a hand on Joe's back. "Don't worry. I'll keep an eye on him."

"Thanks." Joe found the nearest chair and plonked himself down. He hadn't realised it, but he was breathing in great heaving gasps. Excitement coursed through his veins.

What just happened? I'm not sure, but I think I just firebombed a gorilla. That's definitely not something I had on my list of ambitions.

Joe saw Randall making a beeline for him and nodded to the man. "You okay, Joe? You don't look too well."

"Just trying to come to terms with the fact that I just fought in a war against a silverback gorilla and an army of animals."

"It certainly is an unusual turn of events. Not exactly what I was expecting the day I walked into this zoo for a simple business meeting."

Joe smiled. "So, you really paid for this building?"

"The company I work for did, Black Remedy. You've heard of them, of course. It's good business practise to spend a certain amount of profit on community projects or charities. My company seems to have a current focus on investing in zoos, both at home and abroad. Everybody loves animals, I suppose."

Joe laughed. "Ha! I think that may have changed."

Randall laughed too. "I think you're probably right, my friend. Still, we'll ride this thing out. We can settle here, dig in for as long as we need to."

Joe frowned. "You think so? Maybe we can find help outside."

"No," Randall almost shouted the word. "There's no chance. We're the lucky ones. Can you imagine what it's like elsewhere? How many homes have pets? Dogs, cats, hamsters, all turning on their owners. I think we are on our own. Our only chance is to dig in here."

"Okay," said Joe. "Perhaps you're right. It doesn't hurt to hope, though. We have no idea what everywhere else is like."

"You saw the news in the staff room when all this started. It took everyone by surprise."

"Fine," said Joe. "I don't want to argue. You're probably right anyway."

"I usually am," said Randall smugly. "Don't worry, Joe. I will get us through this."

Randall walked away and Joe pondered the man's words. *You'll get us through this? Who put you in charge of everybody's welfare? I don't care what you say, Randall, I have to believe that there is more to hope for than life at this zoo. There must be other survivors.*

"Joe."

Joe spun around. Grace was awake. He hurried over to her, pulling up a nearby chair. "Grace, you're awake. How are you feeling?"

Her eyes fluttered, unable to open fully. She tried her best to focus them on Joe and smiled when she saw him close. "Joe..."

"What is it?"

"I really need...my pills."

Grace was still pretty out of it. Joe went and got her some water. He lifted her head up from the cushions and tipped a small amount into her mouth. She swallowed and a spark of consciousness returned to her eyes. A couple minutes later, she was fully awake.

"Thanks," she said, taking another sip.

Joe cut straight to the point. "What pills do you need?"

Grace turned her head away. "They're in my bag."

"Okay, great. Where's your bag?"

"By the snack machines."

"What snack machines?"

"The ones downstairs. Where you saved me."

"Oh. Well, we can't get those. There's no way."

"I know." Tears began to spill from her eyes. "That's why I'm so scared."

"I don't understand. Scared of what?"

Grace turned her head and looked him in the eyes. She looked terrified. "I'm scared of hurting myself."

Joe scratched at his head. His hair felt flat and greasy. "Why would you hurt yourself?"

"Because that's what I do when I don't have my pills."

Joe sighed. "You're really gonna have to make this easier for me. What do you need the pills for? Are you ill?"

More tears filled her eyes. "Yes. I have OCD."

Joe shrugged. "Doesn't that just mean you have to be really clean or something?"

"For some people it is. OCD causes compulsions, but I don't get urges to clean, I get urges to--"

"Hurt yourself." Joe was starting to understand and he didn't like it.

"It'll get worse and worse. It'll drive me insane until I start slicing myself to stop the urges."

"That's what happened to your arm, isn't it? That's why you were in a room alone when the scorpions attacked."

Grace shut her eyes tightly and salty liquid ran tracks down her cheeks. "I found some scissors. I was cutting myself when the scorpions appeared."

"What if we get rid of all sharp objects?"

Grace laughed. The sound was hollow and broke Joe's heart. "You mean take away everyone's weapons when we're being attacked by a zoo full of animals? I don't think so. Besides, I'll find a way. Even if it means biting chunks out of myself."

Joe cringed at the image of her eating her own flesh. He didn't know such conditions existed. Grace seemed so normal.

"I'll make sure nothing happens to you," he said earnestly. "Even if I have to watch you twenty-four-seven. You're my friend. We'll get through it together."

Grace smiled again. This time it seemed a little more heartfelt, but Joe could tell that he had done nothing to allay her fears. She was terrified.

Joe stood up, but not before leaning forward and kissing her on the cheek. "I'm just going to check on Danny," he said. "I'll be right back. If you need me I'm just a few feet away."

Once he was happy that Grace would be okay for the time being, Joe left her to rest. By the room's window, Danny was on his tiptoes and hanging over the ledge. Joe shouted at him to get down.

"Dad, you need to see this. They've all gone."

Joe slid up beside his son and looked out. There was no sign of the animals, other than a few burnt llama husks and some unidentified stains on the pavement. Mostly all that remained was trampled grass and scorch marks from the firebombs. The attack was over.

For now...

Victor stood nearby, checking over the remaining firebombs and weapons. Joe approached him. "You think we'll need those?"

"Who knows, but a retreat in battle does not mean the war is over."

Joe nodded. "They could come back."

"Aye, and likely they will. But we beat them once and we can beat them again. We proved today that we're far from toothless."

Joe offered his hand to Victor. "We should all thank you for getting us organised."

Victor did not take his hand. "We did our jobs. If you're gonna thank anybody, thank yourself for doing what was required of you."

"Okay," said Joe, reeling back his arm. "I'll leave you to it, then. Just one last thing?"

"What?"

"How long do you think they'll be gone for?"

Victor thought for a moment then shrugged. "No idea. Maybe a day."

Joe nodded and took a deep breath. "That's good to hear."

"Why?"

"Because it will give me time to go downstairs."

CHAPTER 21

JOE COULD SEE Bill wasn't happy with his plan. "You're crazy," he said. "You can't go down there!"

Joe leant in close. "Look, I just have to, alright? Grace is ill and I need to get her medication."

Bill shook his head. "What's wrong with her? I'm sure Mason would be able to find something to help in one of the labs."

Joe wished it were true. "I can't say what's wrong with her, but if I don't get her pills then she's really going to suffer."

Bill didn't answer. He just kept shaking his head.

"Look," said Joe. "We all have to stick together. Grace needs my help. I'll feel better knowing she's safe. Wouldn't you?"

"What about Danny? Is he going to be safe if you get killed down there?"

It was something Joe couldn't think about right now. If he did, he wouldn't be able to do what was needed. "I don't intend to die down there. I'm not insane. The animals have retreated for now. It will be safe. This might be my only chance."

Bill took a deep breath and scratched at the salt-n-pepper stubble on his chin. "Okay, then I'm coming with you."

"What? No way. There's no reason for us both to take a risk."

"I thought you said it would be safe?"

"Yeah...probably...most likely."

Bill grabbed a litter spike from a nearby table and held it up like a spear. "Then there's nothing to worry about."

Joe had no argument. He picked up his own litter spike and prepared to get going. The quicker he got this whole thing done, the better. Danny would be fine left with Mason, but Joe didn't think the man was particularly experienced in minding children. It would be unfair to leave them together for too long.

He headed out into the corridor and Bill followed him. If he was honest with himself, he was glad for the company. There was every chance that the lower floor would be deserted, but that didn't make it any less frightening. Before he even thought about getting downstairs, though, he would have to get through Victor's barricade.

Victor was unwilling to let anyone tamper with the entryway. Earlier, when Joe had first voiced his intentions, the Scotsman had made it clear that keeping the upper floor safe was his only priority. If the animals were still downstairs then Joe wasn't getting back inside the barricade until it was completely safe. If things were very bad then this could be a one-way journey.

"You ready there, pal?"

"Yeah, I'm ready. Bill is coming too."

Victor eyed up Bill and laughed. "Queer and crazy? You're both bloody mad for doing this. Still, you're not prisoners. It's your choice."

"It is our choice," said Bill. "About whom we are and what we do."

"Aye, well, watch your backs out there." Victor nodded to Joe. "You especially, with this one around."

Bill sighed, but let it go as he often did. Like Joe, he was probably just thinking it wasn't worth the aggravation. "Just let us past," he said.

Victor pulled a printer off the top of a desk and slid the furniture aside, creating a narrow gap. "Remember, if I hear a ruckus down there then the barricade stays up. I've already cleared a space for the door downstairs, but I'm gonna block it back up once you've left."

Joe nodded and moved past the stack of furniture. His footsteps echoed as he took the stairs downwards. There were no other sounds, though, and Joe started to relax as it appeared more and more likely that the coast would be clear. The barricade in front of the staff room door was cleared of debris, just as Victor had said it would be, the furniture having been moved to one side.

Joe waited for Bill to catch up. "You ready?"

Bill nodded. "Whenever you are."

"Let's do it then." Joe pulled open the door and slid through. Bill followed closely behind. The staff room was a mess. Chairs and tables were upturned, the television had been pulled down off the wall and smashed, and the stench of monkey faeces filled the air and covered everything.

Bill picked up a broken pool cue, smeared with excrement, and examined it. "They really did a number on this place, huh?"

Joe nodded. "Stinks like hell."

"All the more reason to just get this over with."

The two men headed for the door that led into the next corridor. As they went, Joe kept a watchful eye on the shattered windows at the edge of the room. A gentle breeze came in through the gap, but nothing else.

Bill opened the door and waited for Joe. They crept through into the corridor and Joe suddenly thought about the lions that had started this whole thing.

Please be gone... Please be gone.

Everything seemed to be clear, the corridor like any other you'd find in a million office buildings throughout the land.

"I think we're good," said Joe.

"Yeah," said Bill. "So far."

They moved quickly, gaining confidence with every step that passed without incident. At the end of the corridor was the dented door that would lead out into the zoo's education hall.

"You ready?" Bill asked.

Joe nodded and they opened the door.

There was so much adrenaline coursing through Joe's system that he almost threw up on his shoes.

Shit, what the hell am I doing? This is insane.

"Hey!" Bill grabbed his arm. "Get a move on."

Joe rushed out into the wide open area of the hall and was horrified by what he saw. Ripped and leaking corpses scattered the floor like a gruesome carpet. Severed organs and dismembered limbs littered every corner. Joe's foot almost slipped as it landed in a puddle of congealing blood. He froze, unable to take another step. The fake animals that lined the edges of the room seemed to glare at him, ready to come to life and devour him. "I don't think I can do this. All these people..."

Bill came around to face him. "Hey, look at me. Don't look at them. We can't do anything for them. My boyfriend might be here somewhere, but I can't think about that right now. Let's just do what we came here to do and then we can get away from all this horror."

Joe nodded and willed his legs to move. Stiffly, he managed to take one step forward, tacky blood trying to suck his trainer back down. The steps after that came easier. Before long, Joe was moving quickly across the room, heading for the snack machines where he had originally rescued Grace. He tried to ignore all the corpses as he stepped carefully over them, pretending that they were something else, just obstacles in his way.

He reached the snack machine and, lying between them like a prize, was a small purple-leather handbag. Joe sighed and clicked the knuckles of his right hand. "That was easy."

"Is it there?" Bill shouted across the room.

Joe flinched. Things seemed safe, but that didn't mean they should raise their voices. He turned in Bill's direction and decided to just nod instead of saying anything back.

Joe picked up the handbag. It was heavier than he had expected it to be but he wasn't willing to look inside. You should never look in a ladies handbag without her permission, his mother had always told him. It was a lesson still ingrained in him today.

Time to go. I got what I came for.

Joe turned around and held the bag up so that Bill could see it. For some reason the other man didn't seem relieved. In fact he looked concerned.

Something snatched the bag from Joe's hand.

Joe spun around to find a monkey sitting atop one of the snack machines. It was one of the cute little white-faced monkeys that you always saw in films. Capuchin, is it? Right now, the animal was far from cute. It was covered in blood and snarling at Joe with murder in its feral little eyes.

"Holy shit!" Joe leapt away instinctively and started to run. Behind him the monkey screeched at a pitch so high it could break glass. Joe stopped and spun around. He couldn't leave without Grace's bag.

"Come on, man," Bill shouted urgently. "Get your ass away from that thing."

"I need the bag."

"Leave the bag. It's not worth it."

Joe headed back to the monkey. It was holding the bag above its head like a trophy, hooting as though boasting some great victory over Joe.

That bag belongs to me, you little fleabag.

Joe decided the only tactic he had at his disposal was surprise. He rushed the monkey and made a quick snatch for the handbag. His fingers found the strappy handle and clenched tight. The monkey pulled back. A tug of war ensued.

"Let go, you bastard!" Joe pulled with all of his might and managed to dislodge both the monkey and the handbag. Both hurtled across the room before skidding on the blood soaked tiles. Joe sprinted towards them.

"Joe, stop!" Bill shouted. "Get back!"

Joe halted, heels skidding in a pool of blood. He looked at Bill and shrugged. "What?"

Lined up in the outdoor entrance were the four lions that had ripped so many people apart just days before. They seemed even bigger than before and even more blood stained their snouts. Joe's spine damn near froze stiff, but he somehow managed to take a slow step toward Grace's bag. Before he could take another, the lions made their move.

Joe dodged to the left just as one of the lionesses made a swipe at him.

"Damn it!" Bill shouted again. "Get out of there, now!"

Joe didn't need to be told twice. He sprinted so fast that his hamstrings felt as though they might snap away from his bone; but he kept the pace, dodging and leaping between tables like a twenty-year old parkour practitioner on the streets of Paris.

Bill sprang forward, litter spike in hand. He aimed a thrust at the nearest lion just as it was about to take Joe down. The animal roared and fell back in an injured hunch, bleeding from a puckering wound in its chest.

Joe grabbed Bill by his arm and pulled him along. The two men dashed for the corridor, dashing through the open red door. Joe could hear the pounding of thick paws behind him and was sure that it was only a matter of seconds before he felt their overwhelming weight bear down on him.

We're screwed.

Bill reached the staffroom first, a few steps ahead of Joe. Somehow, the older man was fitter and faster. Joe barrelled through after him, felt his legs weaken as exertion began to take its toll.

Inside the staffroom, things were even worse.

The monkeys had taken over the room again, teeming in through the broken windows. They were the larger species from before – Macaques; the ones that had chased everyone upstairs on the day it all started.

Joe turned to retreat, but found himself faced with the lions coming up the corridor. "Shit, what do we do?"

"I don't know," said Bill, swiping at whichever monkey dared get too close to him. "We're surrounded."

The lions closed in behind them. The monkeys came at them from the front. They were trapped. Joe thought about Danny – he wanted his last thoughts to be about his son.

"We're screwed," said Bill. "Totally screwed."

"Not yet you're not," came a voice from across the room.

Both men looked over to see Mason at the foot of the stairwell. He was holding something in his hand. Before Joe could work out what it was, Mason had already thrown it.

The firebomb sailed through the air.

It landed smack-bang amongst the monkeys. They shrieked and screamed as the flames clung to them. The smell of burning fur consumed the air and stung Joe's eyes.

"Run for it!" Mason shouted.

Joe and Bill dodged through the flailing monkeys and managed to cut a route towards Mason. The lions stayed back, unnerved by the flames and unable to overcome their primal fear of it. It seemed like an eternity to reach the door, but eventually Joe and Bill made it there. They piled through into the corridor and all three of them immediately set about rebuilding the barricade. During that time, Joe heard the sprinkler system come on in the staff room. The fires would go out. The animals would attack again soon.

Need to hurry.

The barricade was up. All three men let out long, laboured breaths. Joe felt as though the acid in his oesophagus was about to burn right through his chest. Bill looked even worse. In fact, the older man had collapsed to the floor.

It was then that Joe spotted all of the blood.

CHAPTER 22

RANDALL SHOOK HIS fist at Victor, could barely contain his anger. "Why did you let Mason leave? If Joe wanted to take a silly risk than that's his decision, but Mason is an expert on the zoo, and animals in general. Do you not think he needed to be kept out of harm's way?"

Victor's hackles were up and he obviously didn't appreciate being shouted at. Randall didn't care – the man should not have made a decision without consulting him first. There was a chain of command and it needed to be respected.

Victor cleared his throat, an aggressive sound. "Listen, pal! Mason wanted to go after Joe and the queer, and I had no right to stop him. We're not prisoners here. It's a man's own choice to do what he thinks is right."

Randall backed off a little, deciding a different tactic was required. "Of course we're not prisoners, Victor, but you said yourself that if you hear any trouble downstairs then the barricade stays in place. So why did you move it for Mason?"

"I said I wasn't about to let anyone back inside if I heard trouble. I didn't say anything about letting people out. Besides, I guess I changed my mind. Sounded like Joe and the queer needed help, so I gave it to them."

Randall sighed. "And what if all three of them are now dead? Mason's loss will be because of you."

"Fuck that! Mason is old enough to make his own decisions. I'm not his keeper."

"Perhaps you should be!"

"What you talking about?"

Randall placed a hand on Victor's bony shoulder. "Victor, it's just us now. Keep this to yourself, but I managed to make a call on my phone to the emergency services."

Victor's eyes narrowed. "What phone?"

"It doesn't matter. What matters is that when I called 999 and there was an automated message saying that no help is available and that people should barricade themselves in their homes."

"Aye, well that would be sound advice."

"But don't you get it? If there's no police force then what hope do ordinary people have? How many people have dogs in their homes?"

Victor thought about things for a while, rubbing his hand back and forth over the stubble of his head. "Shit, pal. That's grim thinking."

"But realistic, I'm afraid. We are alone in this and we cannot afford to take risks. We need to take control of the situation and keep people safe."

"How the hell do we keep people safe? The world's gone down the crapper."

"By keeping them under control. From now on, no one does anything without me agreeing to it. I'm in charge, for the simple fact that I am the only one looking at the big picture. Everyone else is being far too rash and emotional for their own good."

"And what if people don't want to follow your lead?"

Randall smiled. "That's where you come in, my friend. I give the orders – you make sure they're followed. It's the only way to keep everyone alive. That's what counts more than anything right now – that we all get through this in one piece. It may seem harsh but it's the only way. We need to have control."

Victor nodded slowly. Randall could see the conviction flowing into the man like juice into a beaker. "Okay, boss. I agree. We have to keep everyone in check for their own good. No more running off half-cocked or doing their own thing. From now on, everything that happens goes through us."

Randall patted him on the back. "Good man. They'll thank you for it later, my fri-"

"Help us!"

Randall looked through the gaps in the barricade and saw Mason coming up the stairs, followed by Joe who seemed to be carrying Bill over his shoulder.

Mason cried out again. "Let us through. Bill is injured. We need help."

"Did any critters get through with you?" asked Victor.

"No. We got the barricade back in place. It's safe."

"Bloody better be," said Victor, sliding furniture out of the way.

Mason rushed through the gap and Joe followed, still holding the other man over his shoulder.

"Come on," said Randall. "Let's get him into the lab."

The group of men hurried along the corridor and entered the veterinary lab. Randall noticed all of the blood-stained cages that lined the room, but was impressed that there were no remains of the animals that Victor had slaughtered. He'd even disposed of the harmless birds.

The man is efficient, got to give him that. God knows where he's put all the 'meat' though.

Joe eased an unconscious Bill down onto the stainless steel operating table and Randall saw the man's injury for the first time. The back of one leg was split down the middle so deep that it lay open like a ketchup-filled baguette.

"My word, what happened?"

"I'm not sure," said Joe. "I think he must have got slashed by one of the lions when we were running. He must not have felt how bad it was in all the panic."

"Makes sense," said Grace, entering the room. "Adrenaline does that."

Randall frowned. "What are you doing here, my dear? You should be resting, not getting involved in gruesome things like this."

Grace dismissed Randall with a wave of her hand.

Insolent Bitch!

"I can help," she said, moving up beside Bill. "I have a bit of experience with stitching wounds"

"Really?" said Victor. "How's that?"

"Let's just say I've seen my fair share of wounds."

Randall cleared his throat. "Didn't you learn first aid in the army, Victor?"

The man shrugged. "First aid, yes, but not how to suture a wound like this. I could give it a stab, but if the lass says she knows best then I would say she is the one to do it."

Randall didn't trust what Grace was claiming, but what could he do? If she purported herself as being able to manage the wound then on her head be it. "Okay," he said. "Then I suggest she gets to work before Bill loses anymore blood."

Grace nodded. "The bleeding doesn't seem to be arterial, so we just need to clean the wound and close it to prevent infection. I need someone to get some of the ethanol we've been using for the fire-bombs, and the cleanest cloths we can find. Mason, do you know if we have a suture kit in here?"

Mason nodded and went to the side of the room. Victor headed for the door in what Randall assumed was a trip to go and get the alcohol. Grace went to work on Bill, tearing away the clothing from his wound and then elevating the leg on a cardboard box full of printing paper.

"You obviously have things under control here, my dear. I will leave you to it."

"I'll come with you," said Joe. "I need to look after Danny. With Grace here, he'll be alone with Shirley."

Randall smiled. "I'm sure he's more than safe with Shirley."

Joe huffed. "Are you crazy? That woman is unstable."

"I admit that she is a little...eccentric, but we have no right to judge. We are all part of the same team now and I won't abide malcontent."

"You won't abide it?" said Joe. "You're not really in a position to--"

"Joe, we can discuss it later. In fact, I think it would be best if we all spoke as a group at the next opportunity. For now, it would be best to take my advice and not rock the boat. If we start to bicker amongst ourselves things will fall apart."

Joe shoved Randall aside. "I don't know if you've noticed, but things have already fallen apart!"

Randall waited a few moments and then followed Joe out into the corridor.

As long as there is order, things have nowhere near fallen apart. That is a lesson you will have to learn, Joe, my friend. Whether you agree with it or not.

CHAPTER 23

WHO THE HELL does that guy think he is? Joe couldn't believe the way Randall acted as though he was in charge, strutting along like he was at a business conference and everyone else was a subordinate. They were all in this nightmare together and no one had the right to tell anyone else how to think.

Especially when it concerns my son and that nutcase, Shirley.

Joe found Shirley standing at the window of the seminar room. Danny stood beside her. They were holding hands and chatting amongst themselves.

Joe shouted. "Danny! Come here."

Danny jumped at the sudden sound of his father's voice and twirled around like a spinning top. "Dad, you're okay! You shouldn't have left."

"Of course I'm okay. You don't need to worry about me."

Danny ran over and wrapped his arms around Joe and squeezed. Over by the window Shirley turned around casually and smiled sagely.

"I'm glad you returned safe and sound, Joe," she said. "That's a fine boy you have there."

Joe clutched Danny tighter, running a hand underneath one of the straps of his backpack. "Yes, I know. Thank you. What were the two of you doing anyway? I don't like him being by the window."

"We were talking about the nasty animals," Danny answered. "Mrs. Shirley told me that God has told them to attack us because we've all been bad. She told me about Noah and his boat and that this is the same sort of thing that happened hundreds of years ago, except this time the animals are the water."

"Noah had an ark, Danny," Shirley corrected, "not a boat. Try to remember. Facts are important."

Joe felt his skin glow red beneath his clothing. "Keep your self-righteous bullshit to yourself, Shirley. My son doesn't need to hear things like that."

Danny stared up at him, wide-eyed. Joe felt guilty over his display of bad language in front of his son, but still felt it was warranted. Shirley didn't seem so shocked and took the insult in her stride.

"On the contrary," she said calmly. "I believe it is of the utmost importance that your son learns about the world he has inherited. Of all of us, he is the only one without sin. He is the only one with any chance to continue on in this vile landscape of sin and sodomy."

"Enough!" Joe took Danny away, heading for the furthest corner of the room. "Just leave my son alone, okay?"

"You cannot hide him from the truth and you cannot hide the truth from him. Judgement has been passed and he is paying for your transgressions."

Joe kept on walking. Bloody fruitloop. What world is she living in? Dante's Inferno, by the sound of it.

Danny dove onto a pile of cushions, performing a messy elbow drop like one of his wrestling idols. Joe sat down beside him. "You okay, buddy?"

Danny nodded emphatically. "I'm super-duper... Dad?"

"Yeah?"

"Why were you mean to Mrs. Shirley?"

Joe sighed. How did you explain it to a child? "She's a bit mixed up, Danny, and I don't want her to tell you things that are silly. Sometimes adults can get stuff wrong, too."

"She was just telling me stories."

Joe tussled Danny's hair. "I know, son. Just promise me you won't listen to her anymore, okay? If you want a story then just ask me."

Danny nodded, but seemed to be thinking about something. "Mommy used to tell me stories."

Joe felt a knot in his stomach, tying and untying itself with every breath. "I know she used to. You're mommy was a lovely lady."

Was? Dammit, I should have said 'is'.

Danny didn't seem to pick up on the past tense. "When can I go home and see her? I want to tell her about all of the animals, and how you've been saving everybody. Maybe if I tell her she'll like you again."

Joe thought about that. It had been so long since there had been anything but acrimony between him and Jane that the thought of her being proud of him was alien – but the notion was a comforting one. It was fantasy, though, because Joe knew that Danny's mother was dead. She had to be. No way could she have survived.

"Dad? When can I go home?"

"I don't think we can go home just yet, Danny. At least not for a little while."

"But what about Mommy? She'll be missing me, and she'll be mad at you. I don't like it when she's mad at you."

Me either, son. Me either.

Joe pulled Danny in close across his lap and stroked his soft blond hair. "She'll understand. She won't be mad as long as we keep ourselves safe."

"She's dead isn't she?"

Hearing such a thing from his son – and so suddenly – was like an unexpected punch to the gut.

What on Earth do I say? Is it kinder to lie?

Joe thought about things for almost a full minute before he gave an answer. "Yes, Danny, I think she probably is. I'm sorry. I loved her too."

Beneath his breath, Danny began whispering names, sobbing between each one. "Bulldog, Owen Hart, Andre the Giant, Miss Elizabeth, Macho Man, Texas Tornado, Bam Bam Bigelow, Luna Vachon, Earthquake, Bossman, Yokozuna, Mr Perfect, Rick Rude, Mommy." Joe knew that each name his son said was a wrestling hero that had passed away tragically. And he had just added his mother to that list.

* * *

One hour later, Grace entered the room. Joe sighed with relief. He wanted to know what was going on, to see if Bill was okay, but he wasn't about to leave Danny alone with Shirley again. Now that Grace was here he could find out.

"He's going to be okay," she said before he even had chance to ask. "At least I think so. The wound looked worse than it was and I managed to clean it up and stitch it pretty well."

Joe tipped his head back and let out a long hiss of air before looking at Grace and smiling. "That's such a relief. We all owe you. How did you learn to stitch wounds?"

Grace turned away from him and looked at the ground.

Joe quickly understood. *She knows because of having to stitch her own self-inflicted wounds.*

Grace came and sat on the cushions beside Joe and Danny. She placed a hand on his knee. "I hate to ask, after what you did for me, but did you manage to--"

"I'm sorry," Joe said. "I had your bag, but they..."

Grace's eyes filled with tears and her lower lip quivered. "That's okay," she said. "You shouldn't have even tried. It was horrible of me to even have asked you." She squeezed at his knee. "Thank you for trying."

Joe stared down at the floor, examining each tiny carpet fibre. "I'm just sorry I failed. How did you even know I tried? You were asleep when Bill and I left."

"Mason realised that you were gone and woke me up. I made him go after you, although he seemed like he would have anyway."

"I owe Mason my life."

Grace laughed. "I think a lot of people owe their lives to someone at the moment. We'll have to make a chart or something."

Joe giggled and put his hand on top of hers. "You know, you're the only thing that can make me smile since this whole thing happened. Well...you and Danny, of course."

Grace seemed to blush. "I'm glad. I like it when you smile."

Joe suddenly had a thought that knocked away the levity. "What are we going to do without your pills?"

We? Why do I feel so protective of this girl?

Grace's face sagged. "I really don't know. I've never been able to fight the urges in the past. They've always managed to ruin my life. Even now they're beginning to eat away at me. It's like little shards of glass inside my brain.

"God..." said Joe.

Grace smiled and seemed suddenly hopeful. "But in the past I never had you looking after me."

Joe felt teary again, the emotional hole from earlier not yet fully sealed. He pulled Grace in close and she rested her head on his thigh. Danny slept on the other. Despite everything that had happened, the feeling of their bodies against his made everything feel better. Made him think that things might be okay as long as they had each other.

We need to stick together.

CHAPTER 24

JOE WAS SURPRISED when Bill entered the room flanked by Mason, Randall, and Victor. He had a heavy limp and his leg was bandaged from his knee upwards. Otherwise he seemed okay. Grace had done a good job.

Joe would have stood up if it were not for Danny and Grace's sleeping bodies weighing him down. Instead he raised both hands out towards his friend. "Bill, you're walking about like nothing happened."

Bill smiled. "I've been better, but I'll live."

Victor patted Bill on the back and looked at Joe. "Your lass did a good job."

My lass? Who says she's my lass?

"Yes," said Randall. "She did us all a great service."

Joe scrunched up his face. "Great service? You sound like a politician."

"Perhaps in the current circumstances, I am. In fact that's what we are all about to discuss."

"Discuss?"

Randall perched himself down on the edge of a table. "Leadership, my friend. We need to put some rules in place if we have even a slim chance of making it through."

Joe sighed and shook his head. "Let me guess: you're putting yourself forward?"

"Not at all," said Randall. "I suggest a democratic vote. What other way is there?"

"How very noble."

Randall smiled at Joe as if they were best friends. "I will of course put myself forward as a candidate. With my business background and age I feel I would be best suited to the job, but of course that is for everyone else to decide."

"Do we have any other volunteers?" Grace asked, pulling her head away from Joe's lap, not asleep like they had assumed.

"Not yet," Randall told her, looking down at her position on Joe's lap with what looked like disapproval. "Now would be the time for people to put themselves forward."

"I think Mason should be in charge," said Joe. "He's educated and an expert on animals. Plus this is his zoo."

"And it's my building," said Randall, "but I digress. I think Mason would be a wonderful candidate."

"Except for the fact that I am not volunteering," Mason said. "I'm not cut out to make decisions. I'm a scholar; comfortable alone in a room full of books. I don't wish to have that responsibility."

Joe deflated. The only respectable contender against Randall for leadership would have been the zoo's curator. Without Mason, who else was there?"

"I put forward Joe," said Bill, trying to take the weight off his injured leg by sitting on a pile of cushions. "He's a risk taker, but he always does what's right."

"I agree," said Grace. "He's done nothing but put other people first since this whole thing began."

Randall smiled, the expression drenched in condescension. "My dear, Joe has a son to look after, and that would only compromise his ability to lead. I very much doubt that he would want to-"

"I volunteer," said Joe, cutting Randall off mid-patronisation. "Politicians have children and families."

Randall sighed. "Okay then. We have two candidates. Is everyone ready to vote?" He looked down at Danny, sleeping soundly, and added, "Over-eighteens only, of course."

Everyone sat patiently while Victor used a marker to scrawl the words JOE and RANDALL on the seminar room's whiteboard.

"Okay," said Victor. "I'll chair the vote and ask you one by one to give me your choice between Joe and Randall. We'll start with you, Shirley."

Shirley nodded and allowed herself to think. Joe suspected it was just for show and was not surprised when she answered. "I pick Mr. Randall."

"Okay," said Victor. "How about you, Grace? Should I even bother asking?"

"Joe is the best man by far."

"Thanks for that, lass." Victor drew a scratch below each of the names on the board.

A tie so far.

"I vote for Joe too," said Bill before he was even asked. Joe nodded a silent thanks to the man.

"Hold your horses," said Victor. "I'm in control of this thing, so let's speak when spoken too, yeah?" Despite his assertions, Victor put another scratch below Joe's name. He then put another one beneath Randall's.

"Hey," said Grace. "What's that for?"

"That's for my vote, lass. We have a tiebreaker. Mason it falls to you."

Joe smiled. It's in the bag. No way is Mason going to vote for that egotistical prick.

"I vote for Randall," said Mason, seeming to choke on the words as they came out of his throat.

Grace leapt to her feet and threw out her arms. "What? How can you not vote for Joe? We wouldn't be here if it wasn't for him."

"I'm aware of that. Although earlier I saved his life in return, so perhaps that makes us even."

Joe shook his head, genuinely shocked. "Why, Mason?"

Mason couldn't look him in the eye. "I don't want to see anyone else get hurt, and as Bill said earlier, you're a risk taker. I think things will be a little more stable if Randall makes decisions. And after all, this is his building."

"Bullshit!" Grace screamed at him. "You're a spineless bastard. He said something to make you vote for him, didn't he?"

"Now, now, Grace. I do not wish to hear any talk of corruption." Randall wagged his finger back and forth. "Not under my regime."

Grace cackled. "Regime? There're five people here, you big-headed prick. You're not the prime minister! You're just a sad little man that wants to be in charge of all the toys because no one will play with him otherwise."

Randall turned to Victor. "Control her, please."

Victor shot forward and twisted Grace's arm behind her back. She squealed.

Joe rushed the Scotsman, ready to take him down, but, before he knew what happened, something cracked against the bridge of his nose. He staggered backwards, blood and snot flowing between his fingers. When he looked up, through blurry eyes, he could see that Victor was holding Martha against Grace's throat. He'd smacked Joe in the face with the thick handle before turning the blade on his hostage.

"What the hell are you doing?" Bill shouted, hands on top of his head.

Randall held a hand up like he was talking to a church full of worshippers. "My first order of business is about the adherence to law and general obedience of the group. Victor is now the group's Marshall and will deal forcefully with any disruption. From now on he will also be the only person with access to weapons. I took the liberty earlier of dispensing most of them to a secure place."

Joe spat bloody-mucous onto the floor. "And why did you do that if you didn't know you would get the vote?"

Randall let a smarmy grin creep onto his face. "It was just a precaution. A shrewd one, I believe. Victor will now escort Grace to my office until she calms down."

"What happened to this being a democracy?" said Joe, still blinking tears from the blow to his nose.

Victor answered on Randall's behalf. "The vote was democratic. Now that it's been dealt with, consider this a dictatorship. It's for your own good."

"Indeed," Randall seconded.

Victor strong-armed a protesting Grace through the door and out into the corridor, disappearing a moment later. Bill limped up to Joe and stood beside him, facing down Randall. "You're not going to get away with this!" he vowed.

"With what?" Randall scoffed. "I was voted in lawfully and am leading as I see fit. It is for your own good. With time you will learn to love my regime. I'm certain of it. And if not then you will most definitely respect it."

Joe took Bill away from the scene. He could see the man was ready to explode. "Come on, Bill, we'll deal with him somehow. Let's not worry for now."

"I hope that's not conspiring I hear, gentlemen. I take a very dim view of plotting."

Joe glared. "Oh, don't you worry, Randall. We'll play up to your delusions for now, but just remember that when the situation comes that you need our help, you won't get it. As far as I'm concerned, it's just a matter of time until you fall on your fat ass."

"Perhaps, but until then you will do as I command, or face the consequences."

Joe nodded. "Fair enough."

But sooner or later I'll make sure that the consequences are for you....my friend.

CHAPTER 25

THINGS ARE COMING along nicely, Randall told himself. The group was under control and would be obey his commands. If they did not, Victor would happily show them the error of their ways.

After making an offer that Mason could not refuse, and with Bill being injured, there was now only Joe to worry about.

But there are plenty of options to make that over-sized brute behave. Like his son, or the girl.

Speaking of the girl, Randall thought he should go see her and explain what was expected of her, going forward. It would not do to have her kicking up a fuss again. It was bad for morale.

He crossed the room and exited into the corridor. Victor was coming back the other way, jangling a set of keys between his fingers. When he saw Randall, he handed them over.

"Everything under control?" Randall asked.

"Aye, she's sitting pretty in your office. Feisty one, that lass."

"Isn't she just. I'm going to have to keep an eye on her. In fact I'm going to go see her right now."

Victor nodded. "I'll look after things until you get back."

"Good man!" Randall walked away. The door to his office was locked and he used the keys to open it. When he open the door, Grace rushed at him. A swift backhand soon put her in her place.

She fell to the floor, palm against her bleeding lip. "You bastard!" she hissed.

Randall placed himself down on a swivel chair up against the room's desk. He folded his hands in front of himself and placed them in his lap. "Listen here, young lady. You better get used to the way things will be running around here or else you're going to find yourself locked up more often than not. Things here are very delicate and it would be best if you let the grown-ups handle things."

Grace climbed back to her feet and scowled at him. "You have no right!"

"I was given the right by a vote."

"A vote you fixed."

"Such accusations will not be tolerated – especially ones without substance. Now, if I hear such things again, I will see that you spend an entire week in here alone."

The girl's eyes grew wide with fear and Randall had to fight the urge to gloat that his threat had subdued her.

"You can't leave me alone in here. Please," she said. "You have to let me out."

Randall's thin lips stretched wide. "Not until you learn how to behave, young lady."

"I'll behave," she cried. "Just don't lock me up."

Randall thought for a moment. *What on Earth has taken the fight out of her so quickly? Surely it can't just be the threat of incarceration? Either way, it's a lot of fun watching her beg. Maybe I can even get her on her knees.*

"Why are you so afraid of being locked up, my dear?"

Grace looked away, avoiding his attempts to make eye contact. "I... just don't like being alone."

"Then perhaps a day alone will be a suitable enough punishment to teach you some respect."

Grace lunged across the desk, the act so ferocious that Randall was in awe of how quickly she was upon him with her hands around his throat. He grabbed a fistful of her hair and pulled her back, slamming her down onto the desk and pinning her. He moved his face close to hers, their noses only centremetres apart. "Now listen here, sweetheart. There's a new mayor in town and you better learn real fast to respect him. You hear me?" He yanked harder on her hair and she yelped. Tears spilled from her eyes. "Now I'm gonna leave you here on your own so you can do some thinking. When I decide to let you out, I hope to see a significant change in your behaviour."

Grace began sobbing, but he cut her off by shoving his tongue into her mouth. She struggled and fought to remove him, but he held the kiss a few seconds more until he was satisfied.

I love it when they fight.

Randall broke away and Grace spat on the floor, wiping her mouth with the back of her hand. He moved towards the door, but turned to face her one last time before he left. "You know, with a mouth like that, I may just make you my First Lady."

Randall slammed the door and locked it, leaving Grace alone with her tears.

CHAPTER 26

"WHAT ARE WE going to do?" Bill asked Joe. They were standing over in the corner of the room where Danny was playing with some toy animals from the warehouse.

"I don't know yet," Joe said, "but Randall has no right to behave the way he is. We should just play it safe for now."

Bill nodded. "Or else we'll have that psycho, Victor, on our asses."

"Exactly. That man is dangerous. I don't think he's 'all there', you know?"

"I hear ya. What should we do about Grace, though? We can't just leave her locked up."

Joe bit at his lip as he thought about her. "No, we really can't. We have to get her out."

"Okay," said Bill. "How?"

"Appeal to Randall's decency?"

"Don't think the man has any."

"Me either, but I don't know what else to do."

Bill shrugged. "Okay. Give it a shot."

The timing was perfect because Randall had just re-entered the seminar room and seemed to be in a good mood about something. Joe approached him over by the window. It was still deserted outside, the animals gone.

"Hey, Randall," he said, trying to sound calm and reasonable. "You think maybe you should let Grace out? She's probably calmed down by now."

Randall faced Joe, smug grin attached to his face. "I'm afraid not."

Joe threw his head back, already frustrated by talking to the man. He gave it another shot, though. "It's not safe for her to be alone. Last time she got attacked and bitten."

Randall nodded, as though he was taking Joe's concerns on board, but what came out of the man's mouth said different. "Victor has safeguarded the room sufficiently. He's even added a padlock to the door. There's no need to worry about anything."

"Well, how long do you plan on keeping her locked up? You have no goddamn right! It's kidnap."

Randall folded his arms across his chest. "Don't be so dramatic. She was hysterical and had to be removed for the safety of the group."

Joe saw an opening. "And now she's not, so she should be released."

Randall shook his head solemnly. "I thought just the same thing earlier, but I'm afraid that she attacked me as soon as I entered the room."

Joe looked at Randall's neck as the man turned his head to one side. Sure enough there were red finger marks against the podgy flesh.

So Grace really did attack you? Good for her.

"That's unfortunate," said Joe, "but I promise to keep her under control if you let her out."

Randall leant closer to Joe, eyeball to eyeball. "Let's just dispense with the bullshit, Joe. This whole 'reasonable' act isn't fooling anyone. If I release Grace then it will just add another person to conspire against me along with you and Bill. I'm afraid for now I need to protect the interests of the group. Until I feel I can trust you, that means keeping Grace out of harm's way."

Joe's fists clenched involuntarily. "So, what? You're just going to leave her locked up indefinitely?"

"Don't be silly. I'm a fair man. She'll be released at some point. I suggest you just relax until then, my friend."

Joe walked away before he lost control of himself. Every cell in his body was tensing up with the urge to rip Randall's pig head from his flabby neck. He had to find a way to get Grace out of there before...

Before her illness becomes too much for her to take and she starts cutting herself.

Bill was waiting for Joe in the corner of the room, keeping an eye on Danny. "Any joy?"

Joe shook his head and sat down beside his son. "How you doing, Danny?"

Danny put down a small plastic elephant that he was playing with and looked up at his father. "I want Grace to play with me."

"I know you do. I want Grace, too, but she's busy at the moment."

"That nasty man locked her up."

"He just took her to calm down. She's fine now."

"You're fibbing."

Joe didn't know what to say. His son was smart enough to know that things weren't okay, but was he old enough to know the full truth? "We're going to help her, Danny, and then we're going to get out of here."

Bill frowned at him. "What you talking about?"

Joe looked around the room and motioned for Bill to do the same. Victor and Randall were in discussion by the window and Shirley had joined them. "How much longer do you think things are going to remain civil? Randall is obviously an egomaniacal bully and Victor is happy as long as he gets to stab things. Then there's Shirley; she's a whole other level of messed up. You, me, and Grace are the only ones in this place that see the big picture here, but I have a feeling that our voices are about to get lost beneath the din of 'Team Randall'. We need to leave."

"What about Mason?"

Joe shrugged. "After what he did, I really don't know where we stand with him. He's obviously happy to go along with Randall's circus, so I say we let him."

"I think you're crazy to even consider it. We'll get ripped apart out there."

Joe put a hand on Bill's shoulder. "Eventually, we'll get ripped apart in here. We're not safe, you know that. You're injured. Grace is injured. The animals are chipping away at us one scrap of flesh at a time."

"The animals have gone."

"They'll be back," said Joe. "I'm certain of it. They're just regrouping. Planning their next move."

"Animals don't plan," Bill scoffed. "They don't think – at least not in the way you're suggesting."

"These ones do. You may not have seen the way they worked together to surround Grace, but you witnessed them ambush us downstairs."

Bill obviously didn't want to buy into any of it and he shook his head adamantly. "Just a coincidence."

Joe sighed. He needed to get through to the man. He could make nothing happen otherwise. "Bill, you know that's not true. Whatever caused all this has made the animals act differently, smarter. We need to find help and we won't find it here."

Bill's shoulders slumped and he seemed to deflate. "Where would we even go?"

"That's the part I'm not clear on, but there must be other people somewhere. The army or something. I still have my car keys. We could just drive out of here."

"Well, I'm not on board until you give me something better than that. I ain't going nowhere till I at least have a destination."

"Fair enough," Joe conceded. "Let me think on it. Right now, I'm going to go see Grace."

Bill raised both of his grey-black eyebrows. "How you gonna do that? She's locked in that office. You try to break her out you'll have Victor breathing down your neck – Martha, too."

"Doesn't mean I can't talk to her through the door. She needs to hear that things will be alright."

"You gonna tell her the plan?"

"I thought you said I didn't have a plan?"

Bill laughed. "Well you have an intention. You could tell her that."

"We'll see," said Joe. "You good to look after Danny?"

"As always. He'll be safe with me."

"I know." Joe looked down at his son and smiled. "You okay to stay with Bill for a few minutes, Danny?"

Danny looked up from his toy animals and smiled. "Yeah, he's big and strong like Kamala, the Ugandan Giant."

Joe cringed. "Danny! That's...a little bit racist."

Bill patted Joe on the back and laughed merrily. "Don't worry about it. Everyone's a little bit racist sometimes."

Joe didn't quite know how to take Bill's comment, but the man seemed happy enough so he departed into the corridor. It was getting dark again and the corridor was shrouded in an opaque cloak of greyness. When Joe stood in front of Randall's office, butterflies spawned inside his stomach. The padlock on the door only increased their fluttering.

What if she's already hurt herself? What if she begs me to help her and I can't do anything? While she bleeds to death...

Joe went to knock on the door, but instead placed his palm against the wood. He didn't want to startle her. "Grace," he said softly. "Grace, are you there?"

Of course she's there, you idiot.

A voice came back, weak and trembling. Joe was sure she'd been crying. "Who is it?"

"It's Joe. Are you okay?"

For a while there was no reply, then: "No. No, I'm not."

Of course you're not. Another stupid question for me to ask.

Joe put his forehead against the door, wishing it wasn't there between them. "Is there anything...dangerous in there?"

Grace knew what he meant. "No. At least I don't think so. Randall would have removed anything I could use against him."

Joe sighed. "Good, then you'll be okay."

"No. I already told you!" She sounded desperate. "I'll find a way to hurt myself, even if it means biting. I need to get out of here. The urges are already getting stronger, gnawing away at me. I have to get

OUT!" She banged at the door and the impact knocked Joe away from the wood. The padlock rattled.

"I'm going to find a way, Grace. Then we're gonna get out of here."

"Thank God!"

Joe was surprised. "You think it's a good idea?"

"What? Getting me out of this room or getting me out of this wretched zoo?"

Joe smiled, but realised that Grace wouldn't see it. "The latter," he said.

"I think it's a great idea. I'd rather take my chances with the animals outside than the animals in here."

"What Victor did to you was--"

"I'm not talking about Victor," she said. "I'm talking about Randall."

The butterflies in Joe's stomach flapped their wings again. "What did he do to you?"

A pause. Then: "Not much...yet. But if you don't get me out of this room soon I think he's gonna hurt me a lot more than I could ever hurt myself."

Joe heard Grace begin to sob quietly and a rage started to bloom inside of him.

I'll kill him. That sick, twisted bastard is a dead man. I'll feed him to the lions before he ever lays another finger on Grace.

"Joe?"

Joe broke away from his thoughts. "What?"

"I can tell you want to do something, but don't, okay?"

"He needs to pay."

"Damn straight he does, but I don't want you to go off half-cocked and end up locked in here with me."

Doesn't sound all that bad to me...

But where would that leave Bill and Danny?

Joe took a hold of himself and let out a long breath. "What, then? I just keep my head down until he tries to hurt you again?"

"No," said Grace. "You need to go away and figure out what to do. Then you come rescue me like a hero on a white horse. We'll leave Randall to his playschool prime minister act and find ourselves someplace safe."

"I'm glad you're so confident. I don't even know where we can go to."

"You'll figure it out," she said. "Now go."

Joe put his hand against the door again, wishing he could feel the warmth of her cheek instead of the lifelessness of the wood. "Okay. I'll go figure something out."

He walked away. Before he got far, Grace called out to him. "Joe?"

"Yeah?"

"Please don't take too long, or there may not be much of me left to save."

The thought filled Joe with dread. He walked away without any idea what to do.

CHAPTER 27

NIGHT HAD FALLEN and Joe still had little idea what to do about Grace – or where to go afterwards. For now, he decided to let things lie in his mind, hoping that inspiration would strike unprompted.

Since the day's earlier events, two camps had clearly divided. Over by the window sat Randall and his cohorts, lit by flickering candlelight, while on the opposite side of the room, in near total darkness, sat Joe, Bill, and Danny. Mason sat midway between both parties, obscured by piles of open books that lay around him. The thing that Joe noticed most of all was that all of the food supplies were on Randall's side of the room and that each of his group had weapons. They were laughing amongst themselves, snacking on crisps while Joe's group starved.

They're the elite and we're the proletariat, but I think there's a revolution in the cards for the near future, so just enjoy your cosy little throne for now, Randall. Enjoy it because I'm gonna make you eat it.

Bill whispered beside him. "I've been trying to work Mason out all evening. He hasn't spoken to either you or me since he stabbed you in the back, but he isn't sitting with Randall either. What you think his game is?"

Joe considered things for a moment. "I don't think he has a game. Despite what happened, I don't think Mason is looking to cause any trouble. I think he just wants a quiet life, which is why whatever Randall said to him was so effective."

"You think that's what happened? That Randall said something? He could have just genuinely thought that you weren't the man for the job."

Joe laughed quietly. "I'm not the man, but neither is Randall, that's for sure. I don't know what happened, but I know Mason wouldn't have wanted this."

"It's pretty fucked up. You figured out what to do yet?"

"No, but I'm working on it. I'll try to come up with something by tomorrow. We need to act soon."

"Shit, man, are we really gonna do this then? I mean, we'll probably die."

"I know, but at least by doing this we'll have the chance to live. Grace isn't going to last long if we don't do something."

Bill studied Joe's expression. "You gonna tell me what the deal is with her?"

"What do you mean?"

"I don't know. I just get the impression that there's something you're not telling me. Like why she needs pills."

Joe sighed. "I don't think it would be right to tell you, but I can say that she has a serious condition and that leaving her alone is dangerous."

"Okay."

Joe frowned in the dark. "Really? You don't need to know anything more?"

"Would you tell me?"

"Probably not."

"Exactly, but if you say that she needs our help then I believe you. I've got your back."

"I didn't know Black people actually said that."

"Word, dawg, for real."

Joe renewed his laughter and punched Bill on his arm. "You crazy fool!"

Bill joined in the laughter. "Now I know why your son's a little bit racist."

The two men eventually settled into silence and Joe was left alone with his thoughts. For some reason he found his mind wandering off and retrieving memories of his ex-wife, Jane – Danny's mother. The regret of losing her was still embedded deep within Joe's soul, and not a day went past that he didn't rue the day he had betrayed her with another woman. Yet, in some twisted way, his weakness was the only reason he and Danny were alive right now.

If we hadn't separated then I wouldn't have taken Danny to the zoo for my custody weekend. Who knows where I would have been instead, but the chances of surviving this thing were a million to one in the first place, and if things were different I don't think I would have been so lucky.

None of it made Joe feel any better. He still regretted the past. If he could take back the night he allowed his neighbour's wife to throw herself at him, he would. He would take back the entire last year if it meant he could feel the warmth of Jane's arms around him one more time.

But that will never happen. I have to think about the present. About Grace...

Suddenly it was Grace's arms that he longed to feel around him and he became resolute that he would rescue her. He was going to break her out tomorrow.

CHAPTER 28

RANDALL COULD NOT sleep – too much adrenaline in his system to even consider it. He was finally in charge, free to do as he wished, and it tasted good. Soon he would look towards bringing in other survivors to add to his empire. He considered the methods he could employ, such as lighting signal fires. It would be difficult and dangerous, but he would find a way. That's why he was the one in charge.

That's why he would be the hero when all this was over.

Or if there is no end to this situation, I will remain in power and help rebuild humanity on this very spot.

Randall got up in the darkness and shuffled across the room. He stopped when he came in line with Joe and his group. There was no light in that part of the room, but he could hear each of them snoring, the boy the loudest. The last thing Randall needed now was another inane discussion, which was why it was such a blessing that none of them had woken as he padded out into the corridor and switched on his torch.

Joe is turning out to be quite the problem. I may be forced to deal with him. I know he's plotting something. Him and that bloody queer.

Randall approached the door to his office. Slowly, he inserted the key into the padlock. Despite his efforts to remain quiet as he opened the door, he found Grace awake. She was sitting at the desk and staring at the back of her arm in some sort of dazed confusion. A heavy layer of sweat covered the girl's forehead and clothing and made her glisten under the shafts of moonlight coming from the barricaded window.

"What are you doing awake?" he asked her.

She flinched at the sound of his voice as though she hadn't noticed him enter the room.

"I said what are you doing?"

Grace still didn't answer. Randall was just about to lose his temper when he noticed the blood. "Jesus, girl, what did you do to yourself?"

Grace stared up at him, still struck by some bizarre fugue.

Randall grabbed her by the wrist and stretched out her arm. Embedded into the flesh of her wrist was a ragged splinter of wood. Blood ran down its length and pooled on the surface of the desk. "What's your goddamn deal? You crazy-"

Grace hissed at him. "Fuck you!"

Randall backhanded her across the face. "Get some bloody sense in you, girl."

He stomped over to the filing cabinet. Unlocked it with his key. From the contents inside he pulled out a bottle of water and a first aid kit. He set them down on the desk. "To think I came in here to check on you and this is how you repay me. Suicide is for the weak and pathetic."

"I wasn't trying to kill myself."

Randall raised an eyebrow as he unscrewed the top from the water bottle. "Just shut up and give me your arm." He poured the water over the wound and the blood diluted pink as it ran down toward her elbow. She winced as the liquid touched her skin and tried to pull away, but he held her tight. When the wound was clean, he put on a plastic glove from the first aid kit and yanked at the wooden splinter. Grace squealed as it came free.

Randall examined the bloody splinter in his hand and felt revulsion as he imagined what it must have felt like entering the girl's flesh. "Where did you even get this from?"

"The table leg was split."

Randall looked down at the bottom of the desk and saw that one of the legs had a deep gouge in it. He took a bandage from the kit and started to wrap her wound. "Why did you do this?"

Grace started to cry. "I can't help it. I need my pills."

Randall nodded. "So that's why Joe risked himself downstairs. You're a nutcase and you need your loopy-pills."

Grace looked at him contemptuously. "Something like that."

"Well, if you promise to behave, I'll let you out. I'll look after you even."

"I don't want you to look after me. Just let me out and I'll look after myself."

"Is that so? Do you not think life would be easier with my protection?"

"Protection from what? Your thug, Victor?"

Randall nodded, the torchlight bobbing along with his movement as he directed it on her wound. "Among other things." He rubbed at the bare flesh of her neck. "I could be a friend to you."

Grace spat in his face

Randall wiped away the saliva with the back of his hand and sprang to his feet. "Bitch! Fine, be that way." He yanked open the filing cabinet and took an object from inside. "We'll see how much longer you can last until you're begging for my mercy."

Randall stormed off towards the exit. Before he left, he turned around and tossed a surgical scalpel onto the floor. It skidded into the centre of the room with a clang.

Grace's expression was one of utter horror.

"Good luck without your pills," Randall said, and then closed the office door.

CHAPTER 29

THE FIRST THING Joe thought about when he opened his eyes was Grace. The night before, he had awoken with her beside him. He already felt her absence like a bedsore. He looked around and saw that everyone else in the room was still sleeping. Danny's little eyes twitched as he no doubt dreamt about being a famous wrestler.

Joe crawled along the floor, gradually raising himself until he was on his feet. He snuck out into the corridor, intending to check on Grace again, and stopped outside the office door when he reached it. He rapped a knuckle lightly on the wood.

Silence.

He knocked again, but still received no response. A fire ignited in his belly. Come on, Grace, answer!

Joe knocked one more time, a little louder this time but still quiet enough not to risk waking the others.

"Joe, is that you?"

"Grace! Are you okay?"

That stupid question again.

"I...I'm alive and that's what matters."

"I'm going to get you out of there, right now. This has to sto-"

"Joe, listen to me."

Joe stopped what he was doing. "What is it?"

"It's Randall. He came in last night and--"

Joe bashed his fist against the door. "That fucker!"

"No, no, nothing happened. Nothing like that."

"Then what?"

"He opened a filing cabinet in here to...to get me a bottle of water. He forgot to lock it when he left."

"Okay, and...?"

"It's full of supplies. Food, weapons, medicine."

Joe cursed under his breath. "That dirty, rotten--"

"But that's not the thing that really matters. I found a phone in the cabinet. There're messages on it about government rescue centres. There's one down the road – in Leicester."

Joe's eyes stretched wide. "You're kidding me?"

"You have to tell the others. They won't support him if they know he's been holding out on us all."

"You're right," Joe agreed. "We'll have you out of there in a jiffy."

"A jiffy?"

Joe blushed. "That's what I said. Just hold tight for a little while longer, okay?"

"Go do what you have to do, Joe. Just don't forget about me, okay?"

Joe smiled and ran his fingers against the door's surface. "Never."

He turned around and hurried back towards the seminar room. The weight of the information Grace had just given him was almost sending him dizzy.

I can't wait to see your face, Randall – you arrogant asshole. I knew it would only be a matter of time until I brought you down. Turns out that your little reign of terror isn't even gonna last a full day.

Joe had a smile on his face as he pushed open the door to the seminar room. He hadn't expected to be confronted with Randall's ugly face quite so soon, but the man stood before him now, blocking his path.

"And what exactly are you doing wandering around? No one goes anywhere without my express permission."

Joe laughed in the man's face. "Screw you, Randall."

Randall shook his head as if some deep regret had found its way into his soul. "How very disappointing. I was hoping that I wouldn't have to detain anybody else."

"The only thing you're going to detain is my fist in your face."

"I think Victor will feel differently."

Joe smirked. "You think so? What about after I show him what's inside your secret filing cabinet."

Randall suddenly went pale, like an overweight ghost. "What... what are you talking about?"

"You forgot to lock it during your late night visit to Grace. She found your little stockpile, and – more importantly – she found your phone. We know that there's help nearby."

Randall laughed heartily, although Joe wasn't buying it. "She tell you that, did she? The woman's a nutcase. I found her slashing herself to pieces. If I hadn't checked on her she'd probably be dead by now."

Joe felt sick. "Is she okay?"

Randall shook his head. "Not really. I bandaged her as best I could, but she's a very sick young lady."

"I know," said Joe.

"It's a good thing I was there, my friend."

Joe nodded. "It certainly was, you're a hero, but may I ask you one thing?"

"Of course?"

"Why exactly were you visiting Grace in the middle of the night while everyone else was asleep?"

Randall's pale cheeks suddenly went red. "I...well, I..."

"Wrong answer." Joe let loose with a right-handed punch, sending Randall sprawling onto the carpet. He was pretty sure the blow broke the man's nose and it almost felt like payback for when Victor had broken his.

He's lucky that's not all I'm gonna break.

Randall fell down on his rump and squealed. "That is it! Victor, lock this maniac up before he hurts anybody else. I will deal with him later."

Joe looked up and saw Victor approaching from the seminar room. He also saw that everyone else had now woken up and were milling about the room with looks of concern on their faces.

Victor looked down at Randall, clutching his bleeding nose, but didn't seem to care much. "We have bigger things to worry about right now, pal. The animals are back."

CHAPTER 30

JOE KNEW THEY would come back, but he had been hoping for more time. It didn't change things, though. He was still getting out of there today.

Everyone lined up against the seminar room's cracked window, looking out at the horrors below. The silverback had returned, bringing with him an army that dwarfed his previous one. Now cats, dogs, foxes, and badgers mingled amongst the more exotic species of the zoo. A number of the original army's members, such as the African elephant, were sporting wounds and horrible burns – mementos of their earlier, failed attack.

Doesn't look like it fazed them much.

Victor picked up a firebomb. "Same procedure as before, people. The silverback is the priority."

"What's the deal with him anyway?" asked Bill. "Who put the gorilla in charge of all the animals?"

Mason cleared his throat, removed his spectacles and rubbed them on his shirt. "His name is Nero, a very intelligent Eastern Lowland Gorilla. He's the oldest animal at the zoo – forty-eight. He was born here."

Bill shook his head. "Damn, he's been caged here for fifty years?"

Mason nodded. "Yes. Perhaps that's why he's in charge. Maybe he hates us the most."

"Don't matter none now," said Victor, handing out weapons and the remaining firebombs that he had removed from a locked cabinet. "An enemy with a cause is still an enemy. We spread 'em with fire and use the ballast against anything that gets to close."

Joe took two firebombs that were handed to him and thought about smashing them in Victor's face. He knew it wouldn't be the smart thing to do right now, though. The animals were the biggest danger and they all needed to fight together.

Joe had a thought. "Victor, we need to let Grace out. She can fight for us."

Victor considered it. "I agree, but Randall's the one with the key."

The floor vibrated as the animals rushed the building. Joe looked out to see several elephants and a pair of rhinos heading towards the walls. Dust began to fall from the ceiling, coating everything in a film of chalky powder.

"They're gonna bring down the building," said Bill.

"They tried it before," said Victor, "and failed."

The building shook upon impact and Joe almost fell to his knees. "There're more of them this time."

Victor smiled. "Just means more of them to kill." The Scotsmen hung himself out of the window and let loose another beaker of acid. It doused the animals below and they roared in agony – but carried on attacking.

"It's not working," said Joe, lighting the wick on a firebomb.

"Hit them with the fire," said Victor. "Anything with flesh burns."

Joe tossed his bomb through the window and watched it plummet toward the ground. It smashed against the flank of one of the elephants, sending it wheeling around in agony as the flames engulfed it.

What happened next demoralised everyone.

The elephant on fire lifted its snout into the air and angled it over its back. A sudden gout of water released from its trunk.

Joe watched the flames disappear. "They're carrying water in their trunks. They planned for this."

Victor was grinning madly. "Looks like we have a proper fight on our hands, lads."

Bill was in full blown panic now, both his hands on top of his head as he chewed ravenously at his lower lip. "What the hell do we do?"

Victor threw a beaker full of acid and it hit the partially-burned elephant in the face. It staggered backwards, falling to its knees. Smoke hissed from the surface of its skin as globs of grey flesh fell from its face. A moment later the pachyderm fell to the floor, dead.

Victor turned around. "Let's die fighting."

"Screw that," Bill shouted. "We need to get out of here."

Victor thrust his knife at Bill, holding Martha just inches from his nose. "No one leaves without Randall's say so."

Another impact hit the building. Joe shoved Victor's arm away from Bill's face. "Screw Randall! He's been holding out on us all. He has a phone and knows about a rescue centre nearby."

Victor didn't seem impressed. He turned and threw another acid bomb out the window. "Desperate times call for desperate measures, pal. I'm sure he had his reasons."

Joe shook his head in disbelief. "Don't you care? We could find help out there, the army even."

"I know all about how the army works, pal. I'd rather take my chances here."

Joe threw his hands up. "Fine. Have fun going down with the ship, but we're going. Come on Bill."

Joe started to leave when he realised that Bill was not following, instead he was staring out of the window with bug eyes. Shirley and Mason were staring too. Joe turned to see what they were all looking at.

"Holy shit!"

"Aye," said Victor. "Quite a sight, ain't it?"

Coming towards the building was a herd of giraffes. Covering their backs like flies was a legion of monkeys. Joe understood immediately what was happening. "They're going to climb up the giraffes to get in."

"Just like using a siege tower to breach a castle wall," Victor marvelled. "Beautiful."

Joe grabbed Bill and pulled him away from the window. "We're getting Grace and Danny and leaving. Right now!"

Bill snapped out of his daze and allowed himself to be ushered away. "Okay," he said. "Where is Danny?"

Joe stopped in his tracks and examined the room. Danny was gone, his pile of plastic animals the only indicator that he had ever been there. The next thing Joe noticed made him feel sick.

Randall was missing too.

"That bastard has my son!"

Bill looked confused. "Huh? You don't know that. Why would he snatch Danny?"

Joe growled. "Because I know what he's been up to, and like any politician he'll do whatever it takes to shut me up." Joe suddenly had a worrying thought. "Grace, too."

"What are you talking about?"

Joe shook his head and grabbed Bill's arm again. "Doesn't matter, but we have to go."

Joe sped into the corridor, Bill limping behind. He had a bad feeling. A really bad feeling.

Joe didn't knock on the office door this time. He threw himself at the wood. It didn't break, and the impact made him see stars as he bounced off and fell to the ground.

Bill reached down and helped him up. "I don't think a door like that is gonna give."

Joe leapt up and hit the door again and again.

The wood was too thick and Joe slumped against it in defeat. His shoulder was numb, but his heart was where the real agony was.

Bill grabbed the door's handle and turned it. The door swung open and Joe fell through onto the floor inside. The shock confused his brain and he lay there, stunned.

Bill entered the room behind Joe. "Always try the handle first, man."

The words didn't reach Joe as they were meant to; they seemed to float into his ears before fading into nothingness. His mind was too chaotic to accept any new information.

The room was empty and Danny and Grace were gone.

CHAPTER 31

"**S**IT THERE!" RANDALL ordered Grace. He pushed her down on a chair in the warehouse's small office. Danny struggled against him, but it was useless. The cable ties that bound them together by their wrists were far stronger than the boy's meagre strength. Randall reached forward and fastened a new set of cable-ties to Grace's wrist, securing her to a swivel chair. Her blood was all over him, not because of anything he had done, but because of all the thick gashes and tender slices she had made on herself with the scalpel he'd left her overnight.

I guess I did kind of do it to her in a way.

Luckily, she had been lying in a pool of her own blood when he'd entered his office earlier and not coming at him with the blade as he had expected. It was easy to get her and the boy down the corridor while everyone else was distracted by the animal attack. His plan was to exit through the warehouse and make it to the next nearest building, or perhaps even find a car. He still wasn't about to go and seek out the government's rescue aid, but had at least come to terms with the fact that the visitor's centre was a lost cause. It would only be a matter of time before the animals breeched it.

Or bring it down all together. Damned elephants!

The only detail he hadn't worked out yet was how to proceed safely. It was a fairly reasonable guess to think that the coast would be clear – the bulk of the animal army was busy attacking the east side of the building. Hopefully, Victor and the others would distract them long enough for Randall to make his escape unnoticed.

"You can't do this," Grace shouted at him. "We don't want to come with you."

Randall pulled the cable-ties tighter and she winced as they bit into her flesh. "What's the matter, sweetheart? I thought you liked pain?"

Grace was weeping. "No I hate it. I fucking hate it!"

"Tough shit! You're going to have to get used to it, and if you don't shut up I'm going to fasten one of these around your throat and watch while you strangle to death. You're coming with me, whether you like it or not, and when it's just you, me, and the boy you won't have the option of resisting me. There will be no one to save you."

Grace didn't speak.

Good girl. Learning so fast.

Randall stood away from Grace and closed the office door. He yanked Danny in front of him on the metal walkway and made the boy look at him. "And I'm gonna be your new dad. How'd you like that?"

The boy tried to pull away. "You don't deserve to be anyone's dad. You're horrible."

Randall backhanded the boy, which made him cry out, so he shoved his hand over his mouth and shushed him. Danny bit his palm. Randall leapt back in pain, yanking the boy with him by the cable ties connecting them at the wrists. They crumpled to the floor with Danny landing on top. The boy started to beat at Randall with his fists.

"Get off me, you little brat!" Randall reeled back his free arm and struck the boy across the head. The small body went limp and fell against him. "Damn it, wake up. We have to get moving."

"You're a monster," Grace spat. "A pathetic monster. You think you're a big man, but you're the type of person that hits women and children. When it comes to taking on men, you hide behind Victor."

"Shut up, shut up, you bitch!"

But she did not shut up. She laughed at him. The sound was cruel and mocking, and made him remember all the people he hated in life, from school all the way through to this god-forsaken zoo.

"I'll kill you, whore."

"What the hell is going on here?"

Randall looked up from his place on the floor to see Mason standing in the doorway. The man's eye's shone with suspicion behind the lenses of his spectacles. Randall took in a deep breath and tried to swallow, but found that his throat was dry. "Mason? W-what are you doing here?"

"I came to grab some more petrol to make bombs. Victor said there was still some left in the warehouse."

"Yes," said Randall. "Indeed there is. How goes the battle?"

Mason shook his head. "It wouldn't be going so bad if everyone hadn't deserted. Victor and I are the only ones left since Joe and the others disappeared."

Randall raised an eyebrow. "Joe isn't with Victor? Where did he go?"

"I don't know. Perhaps he's looking for his kidnapped son?"

"That's right!" Grace cackled from the office. "He's going to kick your ass soon as he finds you."

Randall tried to pull himself free from under Danny's limp body, with no success. "Kidnapped!" he said, laughing despite being short of breath. "Don't be absurd. I caught these two trying to escape."

Mason huffed. "Escape? What are you talking about? No one is a prisoner here. I think you all need to come back to the seminar room. In the slim chance that we survive the current situation, we can discuss later why you have abducted Joe's son and tied up Miss Grace."

Randall glared. *Don't you dictate to me, you pathetic excuse for a man.*

"Have you forgotten what we agreed?" said Randall. "I'll close this place down. I swear it, my friend. Forget about all the money I promised to invest. I'll bulldoze this fucking place and turn it into flats. I'll sell the animals for fur."

Mason was solemn as he spoke. "I'm afraid this zoo is already closed for business. I've realised it's never going to open its doors again, no matter what happens, with or without your money. Thus, our deal is off. I should never have helped put you in charge. You're an evil little man."

Randall felt dizzy. This was not part of his plans. "Look," he said. The pleading in his own voice made him feel nauseous. "I went about this all wrong. Help get this lad off me and we'll go back and join the others."

Mason nodded. He stooped forward to lift Danny away, but stopped when he realised there was a cable tie connecting him to Randall. "I can't get this off his wrist."

"Don't worry," said Randall with a cat-like grin. "I have a knife."

He shoved the blade into Mason's ribs and twisted. It felt good going in between the bones. The warm blood of vindication flowed freely over his hand. Mason sucked in a deep mouthful of air that never came back out again. He flopped forward on top of Randall and Danny.

Randall grunted beneath the additional weight. "Will people please stop falling on me!"

It took several minutes for him to get out from under the pile of bodies and he had to use the gore-soaked knife on the cable tie to get himself loose from a still-unconscious Danny. Finally he got to his feet and stretched out his limbs, trying to regain some feeling.

Right, time to get back on task.

Just when Randall was beginning to feel back in control of the situation, a snarling voice from behind him said: "What the fuck have you done to my son?"

CHAPTER 32

S O MUCH RAGE flowed through Joe's veins that he almost took flight when he lunged for Randall. The sight of Danny, hurt and unconscious, pulled him apart at the seams.

And he knew exactly who was responsible.

"I'm gonna kill you," he screamed, thrusting his arms forwards like pistons. One blow took Randall by surprise, knocking the man backwards. It was then that Joe saw the knife, and noticed Mason lying face down in a pool of spreading blood.

The bastard stabbed Mason. Did he stab Danny too?

Any fear Joe might have had of Randall's knife was instantly forgotten and he rushed forward and kicked the man. The blow glanced awkwardly off Randall's ribs, but was enough to send him reeling back farther along the catwalk. His wobbling frame came to a stop against the safety railing. The knife fell to the floor. He put his empty hands up in front of himself.

"Joe, please. Stop, I surrender."

Joe snarled and stalked after him. "I'm going to kill you."

Randall backed away, slid along the railing. "Let's be grown up about this. Your son is fine. He just fainted."

"What about Mason? Is he just unconscious?"

"Kill that motherfucker, Joe," said Bill, entering the warehouse and seeing Mason's body on the floor. "Gut him like he gutted Mason."

"Yeah," added Grace from the nearby office. "I watched him kill Mason without a second thought. He's evil."

Joe glared at Randall, who cowered like a child. "I think we're all in agreement. Or would you prefer a vote?"

Randall reached the edge of the steel staircase leading down to the warehouse floor and realised there was nowhere else to go. He teetered on the edge of the top step and seemed to hold his breath as Joe approached. "I-I found Mason like that," he said. "I don't know what happened. I swear, Joe."

"Really," said Bill from behind them both. "Then why is Grace tied up in the office?"

Joe saw that Grace was bound to a chair by a series of cable ties and grew even angrier. She was in bad shape, wounded in several places. Joe didn't know if the injuries had been inflicted by Randall or if she'd caused them herself.

Anger broke its bonds and Joe lashed out. He punched Randall as hard as he could, catching the man beneath his double chin and launching him backwards.

Randall's ankle turned and he went tumbling down the stairs. He crumpling into a ball and hit every steel step on the way down, before coming to halt at the bottom, a broken, tangled mess.

Bill managed to snip Grace loose with some scissors and brought her alongside Joe. The three of them looked down at Randall's unmoving body.

"He dead?" asked Bill.

Joe shrugged. "Don't know. Don't care." He turned around and knelt beside his son. "Danny, wake up."

Danny opened his eyes and, after a few moments of heavy breathing, it seemed like he would be okay. "Dad, what happened?"

"You had a bump on the noggin. Do you feel okay?"

Danny nodded and got to his feet. "I feel like somebody done a DDT on me, but I think I'm okay."

Joe hugged him and then looked up at his other companions. "You guys ready to get out of here?"

"God yes," said Grace.

Bill seemed less enthusiastic, but nodded all the same.

"Okay then, let's take things slow. Get armed and keep your eyes open at all times. Any sign of danger and we bolt back inside, or to whatever the nearest safe place is."

"I don't think there are any safe places anymore," said Bill.

"You might be right, but things have gone too far now. We have to go and try to find help."

With everyone in agreement, the group took the stairs to the warehouse floor, stepping over Randall's sprawled body at the bottom. Danny whimpered at the sight, but didn't ask any questions. Joe knew his son was smart enough to figure out what happened to the man.

Once on the warehouse floor, they set about finding some weapons. It was a difficult task, seeing as Randall and Victor had hidden away anything useful in their own private stockpiles. The best they could scavenge was a couple of mop handles and a length of chain that had been wrapped around a recycling cart. Hopefully there would be no need to use the weapons, but if they did, they would not be much use.

Joe walked up to the far side of the warehouse floor, toward a large square shutter. It was electric, but at the side was a crank that could be used to wind it up manually. Bill stood ready with his chain while Grace and Danny wielded the mop handles behind him.

"So, we really gonna do this?" Bill asked.

Joe nodded. "Just as soon as you're ready."

Bill sighed. "Let's just get this shit over with then."

Joe grabbed the crank handle and began to turn. The shutter rose gradually, making a grating squeal as it ascended. Joe cringed at the sound and wished it would move faster. Each rotation of the crank led to the entrance opening by only a few centremetres.

Bill began sidestepping left to right. "Doesn't that thing go any faster?"

"You're watching me turn it. You think there's a better way?"

"Yeah," said Bill, stepping forward. He draped the chain around his neck and kneeled at the shutter. He placed the palms of both hands underneath its edge and gripped tightly. Then he straightened out his legs, deadlifting the shutter like a barbell. It began to rise faster, open now to waist-height.

Bill motioned with his head to the opening. "Who's first?"

Joe swallowed. Time to jump into the fire. He ducked beneath the shutter and re-emerged on the other side. The cold bite of the autumn-air nipped at his cheeks, but was also exhilarating. It felt like he could breathe properly for the first time in ages. Bill, Grace, and Danny crawled out behind him and each of them looked around nervously.

"What's the plan?" Bill asked, scanning left and right. "I don't wanna just stand around. We're too exposed."

"I've got the answer," said Joe, dangling a set of keys from his finger. "No reason my car won't still be waiting in the car park."

"Great," said Bill. "How far?"

"Back of the zoo. Quarter mile, maybe?"

Grace put a hand on Joe's shoulder. "Easy...peasy."

Joe grabbed her just in time to stop her falling. He propped her up by her armpit. "You okay? You don't look so good."

Grace shook her head and heaved in a series of shallow breathes. "I...I'm fine. I just feel a little faint."

"Blood loss," said Bill, pointing to the many wounds that adorned her body; some of them were still leaking.

Grace was a mess, caked in blood. Most of the cuts didn't seem fresh, though, and he was confident that any severe bleeding had stopped. "I think you'll be okay," he said. "Are you going to be able to carry on?"

Grace laughed, but her voice was weak and hollow. "What choice do I have?"

"Here, I'll take Danny," Joe said, picking up his son. "You just hold onto this mop handle nice and tight and if you feel like you're gonna pass out, let us know."

"Can we please get going now?" Bill's anxiety buttons were being prodded. Joe could tell by the way he was shifting his weight from side to side and swallowing constantly.

"Okay," said Joe. "Let's get going."

The group of them set off. They were in a paved delivery area around the back of the Visitor's Centre. There were no vehicles around and nothing else of note either, besides a large industrial wheelie bin. There were no animals in the area and Joe didn't hesitate in leading everyone forward. They stuck close to the wall, crouching to keep their profiles low. Up ahead, the building ended and the pavement snaked around to the left.

Joe put a hand up to halt everyone, whilst struggling to keep a hold of Danny in his arms. "Everyone wait here. I'll go check and see if the coast is clear."

Joe put down Danny and crept along the last few feet of wall. He peered carefully around to the left, poking his head out gradually. Joe couldn't see his own face, but if he could, he was sure he would have lost all colour at what he was seeing.

"What is it?" said Grace. "What can you see?"

Joe bit at his bottom lip and looked back at her. "The animals," he said. "They're everywhere."

CHAPTER 33

BILL RESUMED HIS anxious stepping from side to side. "What the hell do we do?"

"I think we can sneak past," said Joe. The army of animals was engaged in the assault against the building. Joe was even sure he could hear Victor's wild battle cries as debris fell from the windows upstairs. Amongst the rampaging animals was a collection of bloody and burned husks of various shapes and species.

Looks like Victor's still got plenty of fight left in him.

"We can't just sneak past," Bill said. "Animals have like super hearing, don't they?"

Joe shrugged. "Some do, I guess. What choice do we have, though?"

No one said anything. They could go backwards and re-enter the building, but would have to face Victor and the assault that was going on, or they could go forwards and face an army of vicious, snarling creatures. They were screwed either way.

Danny pulled on Joe's arm. The boy looked like he had something to say so Joe asked him, "What is it, Danny?"

"We can start a fire."

Joe smiled encouragingly. "What do you mean?"

"We could start a fire between them and us. They don't like fire."

Joe thought about it but Bill liked the idea straight away. "We could grab some more petrol from the warehouse and pour it on the floor as we make a run for it. Then when the animals chase we could light it and...whoosh!"

Joe shrugged. "Good as anything else."

Bill smiled, seeming the most confident he had been since they had decided to make a run for it. "I'll go get the petrol," he said. "I think some of it got left with the backup supplies."

Joe nodded and Bill limped off. He took another peek around the wall and tried to make some mental notes of which areas were best to get across the zoo. The zoo animals roamed everywhere, flanked on all sides by dogs, cats, and other domestic animals. Their main force consisted of tigers, wolves, monkeys, and of course, the leader of them all, the silverback. The giant ape stood almost exactly at the army's centre and was beating his chest in defiance as Victor continued to fight back. Every time the silverback let out a feral roar, another group of animals would surge forward and attack the building. The earlier attempts, involving giraffes, had obviously failed as a pair of the long-necked animals now lay dead on the ground. Their current tactic was to send small groups of monkeys against the walls, standing atop each other in an attempt to create a ladder from their bodies. Joe didn't want to stick around long enough to see if it worked.

Another five minutes passed by without Bill returning. Joe began to worry. It shouldn't be taking this long.

"You think we should go check on Bill?" he asked Grace.

She shrugged. "I guess we could. Perhaps we should have gone with him in the first place."

Joe and Grace, along with Danny, headed back along the wall towards the loading bay. Joe wanted to call out to Bill but didn't want to risk being heard by the animals. When they reached the entrance, Joe called out at a hushed level. "Bill, you okay?"

No answer. Joe's worry intensified. He stepped through the entrance, Grace and Danny following.

"Where is he?" asked Grace.

"He's here," said a voice.

Joe looked up to see Bill standing anxiously before him. At his throat was a knife. Behind him stood Randall. The man wasn't alone. Shirley stood next to him.

Joe shook his head and laughed. "Guess everyone gave up on Victor's war, then?"

"Only a fool would have stayed and fought," said Shirley. "The battle is already lost. Victor is just too stupid to realise it."

"That's right," said Randall. "Shirley and I are leaving."

"Good," said Joe. "Let go of Bill and we can go our separate ways."

Randall cackled, shook his head forcefully. "I'm afraid I can't do that. You see, I was brutally attacked, and until the person responsible is held accountable, I simply cannot depart. Unfinished business, you might say."

Joe's eyes narrowed. "You're lucky I didn't kill you after what you did to my son. If I were you I'd cut my losses while I still had the chance."

"Perhaps you're right. Or perhaps not."

Randall slit Bill's throat so casually that he could have been acting it out in a play. Bill's eyes went wide as dinner plates as he fell forward onto his knees, clutching the bleeding gash that lined his neck like an ever-widening scarf. He tried to speak, but all that came out was the sound of gurgling and a weak hissing sound.

There was a high-pitched keening that Joe realised was himself screaming. He shot forward and grabbed Bill. The man collapsed into his arms.

"Bill, it's going to be okay."

But Bill was already dead.

Joe stared at his fallen friend and was filled with equal doses of an intoxicating need for vengeance and simple regret – regret that he hadn't killed Randall when he'd had the chance. He would rectify that mistake right now.

Joe looked up just as Randall lunged at him with the knife. He managed to make a last second dive to his right and missed being stabbed by a hair's breadth. The hard floor knocked the wind from his lungs.

Randall looked down at him on the floor, knife still in hand. "Time for your sentencing, my friend."

"He's not your friend." Danny ran forward and swung his leg like it was a golf club. His little foot hit square between Randall's legs. "How about a low blow, you jabroni!"

Randall collapsed backwards, shrinking into the foetal position and clutching at his groin in agony. Like a shot, Shirley ran forward and seized the boy, slapping him hard across the face. "You brat! You'll burn in hell."

Joe watched in a daze – still winded by his impact with the floor – as Grace swung her broom handle like a baseball bat. It smashed across Shirley's face with a resounding crack! The woman shrieked out like one of the animals outside as blood began pouring from her face. The blow had shattered her glasses and sent the jagged shards into her eyes.

"I'm blind," Shirley cried out as she staggered around in wild panic. "Help me, I'm blind."

"Get your fucking God to help you," Grace spat.

Joe got to his feet gingerly, going up to them both. Danny cheek was bright red, but he was not crying. "Go find the petrol," he told Grace. "I'll deal with Randall."

Grace glanced down at Randall, who was still clutching at his groin and moaning. "Is he worth it?"

Joe didn't blink. "He killed Bill."

Grace nodded and then kissed him on the cheek. She took Danny away and left Joe alone.

Randall had cottoned on to the situation and took one of his hands away from his groin and held it up in front of him. "Now, Joe, let's be civilised."

Joe spat. It hit Randall on the chin. "You killed Bill. You killed Mason. And I'm figuring you would have killed me and Danny, too. Why exactly? Just so you could get Grace to yourself?"

"Of course not. I wanted to save Grace and Danny from all this. I would have taken them somewhere safe."

Joe laughed so hard it hurt the soft flesh of his pallet. "You mean the safe place that you hid from us all? And what about me? Where did I come in your grand plan?"

Randall wouldn't look him in the eye.

Joe nodded. "I see. Well, I'd say that in your case, your punishment should fit the crime."

Randall eyes went wide. "Don't kill me!"

Joe smiled. "Course not. That wouldn't be suitable." Randall seemed relieved, but Joe had more to say. "You killed two people, so simply killing you wouldn't add up. No, I need to do something worse than just kill you."

Randall started scooting backwards on his bum, obviously searching for his knife but finding it nowhere; it had been lost in the scuffle. He stared up at Joe anxiously. "W-what are you going to do to me?"

"This!" Joe leapt forward and grabbed Randall by his legs.

"What are you doing? Get off me, right this instant."

Joe was beyond hearing Randall's pleas. He almost took pleasure as he gripped the man's left ankle tightly and started to twist. "My son would call this an ankle lock," he said, and then yanked as hard as he could.

Randall wailed as the delicate bones in his ankle snapped. Joe thought about breaking the other leg as well, but decided that one was enough. He turned and walked away. "Now, don't you go following us, you hear!"

"Joe, please don't leave me here. JOE!"

Joe carried on walking.

"You're a murderer. A murderer, you hear me? You're no better than anybody else."

Joe shouted back a reply over his shoulder. "Least I've given you a fighting chance. However slim that may be."

He re-joined Grace and Danny in the corner of the warehouse, pleased to see that they had found both a can of petrol and some matches.

"Is that screaming I can hear?" asked Grace.

Joe nodded. "Randall had a little accident, but he's in no immediate danger. Let's get out of here."

Joe took the can of petrol from Grace and she picked up her mop handle again. Then they all headed back through the warehouse, being sure to avoid the aisle that contained Randall. Joe didn't want to hear any more begging from the worthless human being.

They reached the warehouse shutter and prepared to step outside again....

But the animals had arrived. They had been attracted, no doubt, by the recent commotion and Randall's relentless screaming. So far it was only a small group of chimps and a few wolves, but Joe knew there would be more coming.

A lot more.

CHAPTER 34

JOE GRABBED THE petrol can from Grace and thrust it at the nearest chimps. The liquid sprung from the nozzle and doused the animals head to toe. Without even having to be asked, Grace struck a match and tossed it.

Two chimps went up straight away. Two-legged infernos, their wild screeching pierced the air in spikes of pain. It still left about eight more, though.

"This isn't going to work," said Grace, backing into the warehouse.

Joe grabbed Danny by the hand and followed after her.

The chimps glared at them as they continued backing away, but made no attempts to follow. They seemed to be communicating amongst themselves, arms moving frantically in some sort of monkey sign language. Joe didn't dare take his eyes away from them, feeling that as soon as he did they would attack.

"Should we go back upstairs?" asked Grace.

Joe shook his head. "It's too late for that. We need to find a way to lose them."

"I don't think that's going to be easy."

The chimps seemed to reach an agreement amongst themselves and rushed into the warehouse, hopping and rolling playfully as if the whole thing was just a game. Perhaps to them it was.

"RUN!" Joe screamed at Grace and pushed her into action. Danny ran alongside them as Joe continued to hold his hand. Behind them, the chimps whooped and hollered. They ducked behind a crate of fertilising materials. Grace was already panting with exhaustion.

Joe glanced around the crate and saw that the chimps had spread out and were in the midst of a chaotic wrecking spree, ripping and tearing everything in their sight.

"What's the plan?" Grace asked. "More petrol?"

Joe looked at the petrol can in his hand and thought about it before shaking his head. "Can't risk trapping ourselves inside. We need to keep the exit clear."

"What then?"

Joe shrugged. "Pray for a miracle?"

"Miracles are beyond you," said a voice Joe recognised.

He looked up to see Shirley heading towards them. Both of her eyes had been reduced to blood soaked rags, the woman quite obviously blind.

"Shirley," he hissed. "Be quiet."

Shirley turned in the direction of his voice and snarled. "You cannot silence the righteous. The end times are upon us and your punishment is nigh. Your son will burn in Hell for man's crimes."

In different circumstances, Joe would have knocked the woman's block off, but right now all he wanted was for her to be quiet. She was going to alert the crazed chimps to their location.

But it was already too late.

The group of chimps descended on Shirley like rugby players attacking a loose ball. They knocked her to the ground under the weight of their writhing bodies. Unbelievably, the woman did not cry, but instead seemed indignant at their lack of manners.

"Release me, you foul beasts of Satan. I am not one of the forsaken and I demand that you remove yourselves from my body."

One of the chimps sank its human-like teeth into Shirley's shoulder and her mad vitriol turned to screaming. The noise seemed to excite the animals even more and, within seconds, half-a-dozen of them were tearing strips of fatty flesh from Shirley's struggling body. Her screams grew louder as one of her ears peeled away from her head like foil off a yoghurt pot.

Joe slunk away from the scene, thankful that the chimps were too occupied to notice him. He turned to Grace. "Let's make a run for it."

The three of them crept around the opposite side of the warehouse as quickly and as quietly as they could. The sound of blood-hungry monkeys ripping apart human flesh was, but it meant they were all grouped together over Shirley's body. There was a chance to get out without being seen.

Joe stopped near the warehouse's shutter. Grace raised her eyebrows at him. "Why'd you stop?"

"Randall. I left him lying in the spot we just passed. He's gone."

Grace grabbed Joe's arm and pulled. "Let's worry about that later. We need to get out of here."

As one, they ran out through the shutter and back into the cold air of the loading area. They were immediately set upon by three wolves.

Joe pushed Danny out of the way just as one of the large lupines snapped at his face. Joe swivelled and kicked the animal hard in the ribs. It yelped and fell to the ground. Joe was surprised that it did not get up again.

Must have broken a few ribs.

Grace swung the mop handle that she had thankfully kept in her possession and struck another wolf. It rolled across the floor, growling in pain, before springing back to its feet. Grace swung again but missed.

The wolf lunged. Its jaws clamped down on her wrist. She screamed and shook her arm left to right, but the animal kept a tight hold, biting down harder.

"Joe, help me!"

Joe saw a third and final wolf making a beeline for his son. "Danny," he shouted. "Come here."

Danny ran toward his father, the huge animal bounding after him. Joe ran towards him, but didn't make it in time.

The wolf pounced on Danny, driving his frail body down to the ground, knocking the air from his lungs and ravaging him.

Joe screamed so hard he felt something in his throat tear loose in his throat. With every strand of muscle fibre in his body, Joe barrelled towards his son. Danny's screams made him move even faster.

Joe kicked out at the wolf, so violently that both feet left the floor. His right foot struck the animal in the side of the head. The impact threw both it and Joe into a tumble. Pain struck Joe's leg like a fast-moving toxin and he knew that he had broken a toe.

The wolf lay dead, bleeding from its misshapen skull as it lay prone on the sidewalk.

Joe crawled over to Danny. Tears streamed from his eyes. "Danny! Danny!"

His son began to move.

Thank God!

Joe examined Danny and saw that he was uninjured. The wolf's teeth and claws had caused a huge amount of damage, but it was absorbed by his son's Undertaker backpack. It was ripped and torn to shreds.

"Is it gone, Dad?"

"Yeah," said Joe, stroking his son on the back of his head. "You're safe now."

Grace screamed out from behind him. Joe suddenly realised that she needed his help too.

Joe got to his feet. Almost fell down again as pain shot through his toes like an injection of fire. He gritted his teeth and fought through it. Grace was on her back now, her wrist still trapped inside the remaining wolf's mouth.

Joe's first intention was to kick the wolf as he had the others, but that wasn't possible with his injury. He would need to try something else. He looked around for ideas, but the loading bay was empty.

Except for the petrol can.

Joe grabbed the canister and quickly hobbled to the wolf. It was ripping and tearing at Grace's arm, oblivious to anything else – even

Joe pouring petrol onto the animal's hind quarters. But the petrol would be useless on its own.

The matches. Where are the matches?

Joe scanned the pavement, looking for the small square box that Grace had been carrying earlier. He could not see it.

Then he heard someone strike a match.

Joe looked down to see that with her spare arm – the one that wasn't stuck in the wolf's mouth – Grace had pulled a match from the box that lay beside her. The phosphorous ignited and the flame immediately caught against the animal's dusty, petrol-soaked fur. The wolf went up like a torch, finally releasing its grip on Grace's arm. It leapt back in agony as the fire consumed it whole, blackening its skin and melting away any flesh too fatty to burn.

Joe pulled Grace away from the flames. She was wailing and blood covered her body from head to toe, adding to the caked-on layers of her previous injuries. He held her tightly in his arms and rocked her back and forth. Danny ran over and joined them both, turning the hug into a huddle. Joe loved them both so much, but he was starting to think that he would not be able to protect them.

Despite that, he couldn't help but tell them: "It will be okay. Everything is going to be okay."

CHAPTER 35

RANDALL SOMEHOW MANAGED to hop himself up the staircase to the warehouse's upper walkway. He had watched the entire thing play out. He'd seen Shirley get ripped apart by a gang of goddamn chimpanzees. It was enough to send a lesser man insane. He also witnessed Joe's escape and it pissed him off something rotten.

That traitor doesn't deserve to be walking around like a free man.

Randall looked down at his ankle, twisted and hanging in an unnatural direction. "I hope you get ripped to shreds, you monster."

Randall held onto the safety railing and hopped his way along. If he could make it back to Victor, the two of them could hole up somewhere in the building and re-establish their safety. Then they could think of a new solution to get out of this godforsaken zoo.

That's if Victor is even still alive.

And that he forgives us me for running out on him.

I'll cross that bridge when I come to it. I'm sure I can charm some haggis-eating Scotsman into believing whatever story I choose to provide him.

Doing his best to ignore the agony of his broken ankle, Randall hopped along the walkway and into the hallway, looking down one last time at Shirley's bloody corpse and the chimpanzees that surrounded it.

The corridor was unmoving, devoid of the chaos and noise that existed almost everywhere else. If not for the barricade at the far end, it would be nothing more than a normal office hallway. Randall felt like he was dreaming.

Or maybe that's just shock from all the pain.

The day had begun with such promise. There had been order and a sense of discipline. He had been in control of things. Since then, however, he had murdered two people, been thrown down a flight of stairs, and had his ankle snapped like a twig by a lumbering fool. Things had gotten away from him, and that was unforgivable.

But all great leaders face adversity. It is how they recover from it that defines them.

Randall continued his limping hop down the corridor, heading for the seminar room where he hoped to find Victor. As he got closer, he could hear the battle outside continuing – angry trumpeting of stampeding elephants and the bloodthirsty hoots of an army of monkeys.

Dirty, disgusting creatures.

The door to the seminar room was closed and Randall wasted no time in opening it, balancing on one leg as he pushed. Inside he faced madness. Monkeys leapt about everywhere, tipping over bookcases and tearing the contents to shreds. Tables and chairs were overturned and the large window at the far wall was completely broken, letting cold wind gust in from outside. Randall watched with terror as more animals flooded inside, clawing their way through the window one after the other.

Victor was alive, sprawled on his stomach and crawling toward Randall by his fingertips. The Scotsman was covered in his own blood and gashes lined his body like canyons of flesh. The monkeys tore at his back with their claws, biting into him as though he were a fine meal served to them for lunch. Randall could not believe that Victor was not screaming.

But he was pleading. "Help me."

Randall stood motionless in the doorway. "It's too late, my friend. I'm sorry."

Victor glared at him, but stopped crawling as more monkeys piled onto his back and began ripping at a new patch of flesh. "I'll see you in Hell, pal. Then it will be you who's begging for help, I promise ya."

Randall watched for a few seconds longer while a particularly vicious little critter tore out Victor's throat with its needle-like teeth. Then he jumped back and closed the door behind him. Instantly, bodies began to hit the other side of the wood. The monkeys were done with Victor.

And now they want me.

Randall looked up and down the corridor and tried to rationalise a plan of action. With his ankle the way it was, he could not outrun the monkeys if they broke through. He had to hide.

And I know just where.

Randall hopped further down the corridor and headed for the office he had made his own. The filing cabinet inside was stocked with supplies and weapons.

Not to mention my phone. Maybe I can call for help. The army aren't that far away.

Randall flopped against the office door, almost too exhausted to stay upright. He managed to retrieve the key from his pocket and unlock the office, hurrying inside as soon as he was able. The door would need barricading, perhaps with the room's large desk, but right now Randall just needed a minute's rest. His asthma was taking a firm hold of his lungs and he needed to sit and use his inhaler.

The swivel chair almost tipped over as he fell into it, but thankfully it steadied after rocking back and forth a couple of times. Randall managed to let out a slow, gentle breath and felt a little more in control.

Just one breath at a time. In out, in out.

It was several minutes before his breathing returned to normal. Once it did, he could finally think again. He was safe for the time being and had no reason to rush a decision. He would just bunker down until the time was right to act.

And when I do, there is going to be hell to pay for certain people.

He stood up and hopped over to the window. Between the gaps in the barricade, he could see the animals outside. The silverback was still amongst them. The giant gorilla was celebrating, waving its arms in the air like a crazed lunatic. Randall's eyes narrowed at the beast.

Our war isn't over yet, my savage foe. The leader of the biggest army isn't always the one that wins.

Randall was feeling good. The pain in his ankle was fading to a dreary buzzing and the room was secure enough to give him time to plan. And time was all he needed with an intellect like his.

I'll figure something out. I always do. I just need time to think.

But Randall was distracted from his thoughts a moment later.

By the smell of smoke.

CHAPTER 36

"I DON'T THINK I can go on," said Grace, her face pale from blood loss. The wolf bite and many of her other wounds were torn open and bleeding again.

Joe stroked her sweat-soaked brown hair out of her face, but several strands remained matted to her glistening forehead. "We need to get out of here," he said. "Before anything else happens. I know that you're in pain, but I can't just leave you here to die. Me and Danny need you."

She looked into his eyes, but seemed to find it difficult to focus. "You need me?"

Joe nodded.

Grace forced a smile. It seemed to hurt her. "I don't think anyone has ever needed me for anything."

"Well, Danny and I do, and right now we need you to keep moving with us. Once we get out of here we can find you a doctor, get you your pills. Please..."

Grace put an arm around his neck. Joe took it as a signal to lift her up and he did so as carefully as possible. It still caused her a great deal of agony.

"I...I can't, Joe."

Joe grabbed her, placed both of his hands on either side of her face and forced her to look at him. "You can! You have to!"

"I can't. I'm too weak."

"You're not weak. You've held it together better than anyone else since this entire fuckfest began. If I didn't have you to help me with Danny these last few days, I would have lost it. You've had enough strength for the both of us, so don't tell me you're too weak."

Grace went to answer him, but broke out in sobs. Joe could see how beaten she was. He wasn't sure if he could help her. But if she was going to give up on him, then there was something he needed to do first.

He kissed her – the first woman he'd kissed in years. It was long and passionate. Grace pulled away, but not before kissing him back for several long and delightful seconds. She was out of breath when she spoke. "What was that for?"

"For being the first person I've cared about other than Danny in a long long time."

Grace's face scrunched up and Joe thought he had made her feel uncomfortable. Then she spoke: "Do you smell that?"

Joe shook his head, confused. "Smell what?"

"Burning?"

Joe lifted his nose in the air and tugged in a deep breath of air. He smelt it. Something was on fire.

"You smell it now?"

Joe nodded. "I think it's coming from the building."

"Maybe Victor dropped one of the firebombs?"

"Or maybe he started the fire because he knew he was done for." Joe put an arm on her back and took Danny's hand. "Let's go."

Together the three of them crept back along the wall of the building. At the end Joe peeked around the edge. Nero, the silverback was standing there, still leading his army, but he seemed calmer, almost relaxed.

He's celebrating. The battle is won and he's celebrating.

"Look," said Danny, pointing up at something.

"Danny! Get the hell back!"

Danny got back behind the wall. "I was just showing you the fire."

Joe looked back around the wall and up at the second floor. Sure enough, there were several probing licks of flame coming from one of the windows. Joe couldn't be sure but he assumed it was the window of the seminar room. It would not be long before the whole building went up.

"They're distracted," Grace said.

Joe watched the animals and saw that she was right. "They seem nervous of the fire. Maybe our plan was a good one. Is there any petrol left?"

Grace nodded. "I left the can back there. It's still pretty full."

"Okay," said Joe. "Wait here with Danny. If anything comes, call out and I'll be right back."

Joe sped off back towards the loading bay. He quickly found the petrol can and matches besides the smoking remains of the dead wolf. He picked the canister up, pleased to find it was almost full, and then hurried back inside the warehouse. He eventually settled next to a crate of magazines and brochures for the zoo's souvenir shop.

A half-minute later, Joe had soaked the magazines with petrol and had spilled a generous amount on the floor in narrow rivulets, hoping to channel any flames towards other areas of the warehouse.

He lit a match.

Then he ran.

The flames shot up behind him, the heat pulsating against his back as he sped out of the warehouse. The popping sounds of burning plastic filled his ears until he finally made it back to the far corner of the wall where Danny and Grace were waiting for him.

Joe smiled at them both. "I think I just bought us a diversion."

CHAPTER 37

THE BUILDING TOOK no time at all to burn and within ten minutes the whole structure was ablaze. Joe wondered about Shirley and Victor. If either of them were still alive then they would be trapped inside. He hoped they made it to a fire exit, but Joe knew, deep down, that no one was left alive. The battle had been lost well before he'd started the fire in the warehouse. In fact, he had only been helping along the fire that had already ignited on the second floor. Everyone left inside would be dead for sure.

Except Randall.

The thought knocked Joe back a step as he realised something that should have been clear to him. Randall had been missing. Despite his broken ankle, the man had escaped.

Joe's eyes went wide. "I have to go back inside."

Are you crazy?" Grace shook her head. "No way."

"But Randall is still inside. I can't just leave him to burn."

"He'd do the same to you in a heartbeat."

"Exactly," said Joe, already turning and leaving. "That's the reason why I have to go inside. I'd rather risk death than be like him."

Joe rushed towards the loading bay. When he reached the entranceway he stopped. The flames were everywhere, fierce and consuming. The smell of combusting chemicals filled the air.

"There's no way," said Grace. "You wouldn't even get inside."

She was right. The steel shutter had dropped hallway down and was twisted and molten amidst the flames that licked at its edges. Joe couldn't go inside to help Randall even if he wanted to.

Grace pulled him away. "Come on. He made his own bed, let him burn in it."

Joe looked into the fire a moment longer and thought about what it would be like to burn to death. To feel the very skin peel from your bones as the blood in your veins boiled. Randall was human waste, but no man deserved a death like that. Wherever he was, Joe hoped he made it out of the building.

After that I don't care what happens to the bastard.

Joe allowed Grace to pull him away from the flames, and when she did he realised that the delicate skin of his cheeks was throbbing and tender from the heat. "Let's get away before this building comes down on top of us," he said.

At the far end of the wall, Joe once again looked around at the animals. They were disorganised now and anxious. A great white horse began rearing up and kicking out wildly at a grouping of warthogs that blocked its path. Even after several days of this, Joe could still not get used to the sight of so many different animals grouped together. As always, they were accompanied by the silverback gorilla, Nero. The huge human-like beast was furious at the disorganisation and Joe watched with awe as the gorilla swung a huge arm out and struck a male lion in the face. The big cat cowered and backed away fearfully.

"He's lost control."

"Who has?"

Joe looked at Grace. "The silverback. He can't override the animal's fear of fire. They're retreating."

Grace was excited, but couldn't completely release the worry from her face. "But we used fire against them before and they came back."

"I'm sure they're just fleeing temporarily like before. The silverback will regain control of them eventually, which is why we need to move now while we still have the chance."

Joe looked up at the flames on the second floor. They were not as violent as those in the warehouse, but they had started to take a real hold now and leapt from several windows, arcing several feet into the blackening sky.

Joe finally left the safety of the wall and crouched down as he moved forward. Grace and Danny did the same and the three of them waddled along like they were playing soldiers. The path led off to the front of the building, but the area there was still thick with animals. To the right was a landscaped plot of grass that shadowed the public walkway. The area was lined with trees and foliage.

Joe hustled everyone along. "Get beyond the bushes and keep low. There's an aviary at the end of this path and I'm pretty sure the car park was past there."

The three of them kept low and dragged themselves through the bushes and shrubs. Joe kept glimpsing animals through the gaps in the greenery. He hoped they couldn't see him.

Or smell me. Don't most animals have super smell?

Joe hurried everyone along, fingernails clawing at the moist dirt as he clambered forward. It didn't take long before they reached the end of the grass bank and the path beside it. Joe checked out his surroundings. Despite the presence of many dead bodies – some of them children – there didn't seem to be any danger nearby, but of course he couldn't be sure.

Up ahead was the aviary, as he had expected. It was a long building, lined on one side with mesh fences that fastened to the brickwork at the top. There was no movement inside the cages.

"Keep going, but be careful," said Joe.

Grace moved ahead and Danny crouched along between them. Joe left the cover of the bushes and felt rain on his face – just a drizzle at the moment, but something about the wet smell of the air suggested it would get heavier.

They approached the aviary. Joe was shocked by what they found inside. The varied collection of exotic birds and other rare specimens had been reduced to feathers and bloody pulp. Every single bird had been torn to shreds and partially devoured. Joe saw why: at the back of each of the cages the zookeeper's entrances were left ajar. Something had entered each enclosure and systematically butchered every bird inside.

One of those bloody wolves probably. Least they got what they deserved in the end.

"What happened, Dad?"

Joe shook his head. "I don't know. I think the birds were all normal, so they got attacked like we did. They couldn't protect themselves."

Danny moved away from his father and over to the cages. He reached out one of his little arms toward the dead animals and seemed like he was going to cry, but instead he spoke. "Mrs. Shirley told me the other day that animals don't go to heaven, but I think she's wrong. If you never done nothing wrong to no one then I think God looks after you, so I think they're all in a better place now where they can fly around as much as they want and eat lots of worms."

Joe was surprised by his son's compassion and philosophical contemplation. He hadn't known that Danny possessed such a capacity for emotion, and he instantly felt guilty about it.

He put an arm around his son. "You okay, Danny?"

Danny turned to him and there were shallow tears in his eyes. "Everything is so horrible. I miss Mom, but I know she probably ended up like the birds." He wiped at his eyes. "I'm just glad I'll see her again in Heaven one day, but until then I have to be down here with all of this horribleness."

"Things are going to get better, buddy. We're going to go someplace safe and all this horribleness will go away."

Danny looked at him. "I don't believe you, but I don't want to stay here either."

"Then let's go." Joe held out his hand and Danny took it. The two of them turned around and were faced by Grace. She didn't look happy. "What is it?" Joe asked her.

Grace pointed back the way they had come from. Some of the animals had noticed their escape and were running up to engage them. Leading the pack was a cheetah.

"Run!" Joe shouted.

CHAPTER 38

THE THREE OF them sprinted and Joe felt his knees crying out as his strides struck down at a speed they weren't used to. If not for the head start, the animals would already have been on them.

Aren't cheetahs the fastest goddamn animal on the planet? And here's me trying to outrun one.

Danny held the lead, his young legs combatting fatigue much better than the two adults. Grace was falling back, too weak from blood loss to keep up. Joe kept looking back over his shoulder, hoping she would increase her speed, but she never did.

He was forced to stop and wait for her. "Danny, keep running," he shouted. "Don't stop until you reach the car park. I'll be right behind you."

Danny skidded to a stop. "Dad, no!"

Joe shouted louder at his son and felt awful. "DANNY! GO NOW!"

Danny kept on running and Joe turned around just as Grace came hurtling towards him. "What the hell are you doing," she cried. "Move it."

"They're too quick. They're going to get you."

"Then let them. You and Danny need to get out of here."

"Not without you."

Grace looked at him. She seemed so sad that it hurt his heart to look at her. She kissed him quickly on the mouth then pulled away, holding up her arm in front of her – the one the wolf had savaged. It was bleeding badly and Joe noticed that it gushed in a slow, pulsing rhythm.

Matching her heartbeat.

"I'm bleeding to death, Joe. I'm barely conscious as it is, and if you don't get going, right now, you'll die."

Joe looked up at the approaching animals. The cheetah was still in the lead, but had slowed down, stalking them like a house cat stalks a mouse. It would only be moments before it pounced.

"I can't just leave you."

Grace was crying and Joe realised he was too. "You never left me, Joe. In fact, you were the only person to ever stick by me." She wiped at her eyes and a thick streak of blood stained her face. She fell down onto one knee. "But I'm already dead."

"Grace."

"Just go!" She was meant to shout it, he could tell, but she was far too weak now. "I'll be okay," she said. "I'm happy to die if it means saving you and Danny. Then it will mean something. Not if you don't move this second, though."

Joe nodded, his tears falling thick and fast. He looked around and saw Danny way up ahead. If he left now there was every chance they would escape. If he stayed here then Danny would end up alone. Or worse.

So he kissed her.

And then he ran.

Light droplets of rain began to fall from the saddening grey sky, matching the heavy sorrow that filled his heart. He never looked back once. The sound of Grace screaming in agony as her tender flesh was hooked away by vicious claws and teeth was enough to haunt him forever. He could not have coped with the visual. What made it so much worse was how long the screams lasted. In fact, they never stopped. Joe just ran and ran until he couldn't hear them anymore, trying to ignore the sight of the torn and rotting bodies that littered his path like fleshy paving stones. Joe knew that Grace's beautiful body would soon be joining them.

Danny waited for him at the zoo's entrance. He was leaning up against a steel gate, trying to catch his breath while wearing the kind of mortified look that was entirely unnatural on such a young face – a grief that was far beyond his years. Joe reached him and took a quick second to catch his own breath, enjoying the sensual feeling of the rain hitting his face, and then wrapped his arms around his quivering son. But they couldn't stop and enjoy the human contact. The chase was still on. They had to keep moving.

Joe noticed that the gate was fixed to a swinging mechanism on a set of hinges. He grabbed one of the iron bars and pulled, surprised to find that the gate moved towards him easily. It swung shut against the other side of the entranceway and hit against a metal stopper built into a high brick balustrade. Joe looked around for something to lock the gate with and couldn't believe his luck when he saw a large steel padlock hanging open on the gate's catch. He ran over and pulled it out, then lined up the metal loop of the gate with the metal loop of the frame.

The padlock clicked shut and the gate was secure. Beyond it, the animals were resuming their pursuit, finished with the succulent flesh of Grace's body. Joe kicked at the gate and screamed. "We're done! You hear me? You can rot in this godforsaken hellhole. You're welcome to it."

Lightening illuminated the sky, just as the cheetah hit the fence at full speed. It bounced off onto its back, stunned. The gate held firm. Other animals bumped against it, too, but it was no use. The thick iron was designed to stop animals escaping.

And that's exactly what it was doing.

Joe took his son and walked away, pulling his car keys from his pocket – glad to finally be about to use them. "Can you remember where we left the car, Danny?"

Danny slapped a hand against his rain-soaked forehead. "Please tell me we haven't lost the car."

Joe laughed and patted his son on the rump. "Cheeky sod! We haven't lost it. We just need to have a quick look around."

Joe began to worry slightly that the zoo's gate would not hold, or that some of the animals would manage to vault the high walls on either side of it.

He trotted around the car park, somewhere between a walk and a run, trying to think back to last week when he'd parked the car. Things had been so different then. Getting out of the car with Danny about to visit the zoo was a joyful and exciting experience. Getting into the car and finally leaving the zoo would be an experience that would change them both forever. He just hoped Danny was young enough to place it all behind him.

"There it is, Dad!"

Danny was pointing north-west towards CAR PARK D. Joe followed his finger and spotted exactly what he wanted. Lying amongst the blood-stained wrecks of family cars and tour buses was a dark blue Ford Focus that was undoubtedly his.

"Come on!" said Joe.

The two of them, father and son, sprinted through the increasing storm, heading for the car as though it was the saviour of the earth. Just to be sure that he wasn't dreaming, Joe pressed the lock button on the key fob and almost jumped for joy when the car's break lights flashed. The doors were unlocked.

Danny got there ahead of Joe and flung open the rear door, leaping across the back seats. Joe caught up to him and closed it, then ran around to the driver's side and got in behind the wheel.

The smell of the vehicle's interior was sublime. It reminded Joe of boredom. Commutes to work and trips to the supermarket. Nice, normal boredom. It was so calming, in fact, that he sat there for several moments, just listening to the drumbeats of the rain on the bonnet.

After indulging himself for long enough, Joe put the key in the ignition and twisted. The engine grumbled momentarily and then roared to life. It was the greatest sound Joe had ever heard. "Time to get out of here, Dan--"

The windscreen shattered, cracks spider-webbing in every direction. Danny screamed in the backseat and Joe found that he was doing the exact same thing. The shock hit him hard and fast. Once again his heart was beating like a rapid-fire cannon.

What the hell?

Joe sat still for a moment, listening and trying to sense what was going on. Something had hit the windscreen, but what?

All of a sudden, he knew.

It was Nero.

CHAPTER 39

THE SILVERBACK GORILLA beat at the roof like the car was a toy drum, denting it deeper with each mighty blow. Joe and Danny's ceiling caved in on them, eating away at the already-limited space they had inside.

"It's the big monkey," said Danny, cowering on the back seat.

"I know. Just keep down low."

Joe engaged first-gear and pulled up the clutch. When he was sure he had the biting point he released the handbrake.

The engine stalled just as a blow took out the back window.

"Shit!" After the week of chaos he had been through, Joe almost couldn't remember how to drive. He restarted the engine and kept the car in first gear. He lifted the clutch again but this time stamped down on the accelerator. The car roared like one of the beasts inside the zoo and shot forward.

The handling was heavy and Joe realised it was due to the huge weight on the roof and the wet puddles on the road. The silverback was still above them but had ceased its attack, obviously surprised by its platform suddenly becoming mobile. Joe avoided some nearby parked cars and shifted into second. The engine went quieter as it began to climb the new gear. The vehicle gained speed, hitting thirty in only a couple of seconds. The silverback remained on the roof.

"He's still up there, Dad."

"I know, just stay down."

Joe pulled into third-gear and steered the vehicle toward the car park exit. It was only a few hundred yards away, but Joe struggled to see it through the broken windscreen and the thick sheets of rain beyond it. He picked up more speed despite all of his senses telling him to slow down. By fourth gear he was already doing sixty and weaving between the wrecks of abandoned cars.

The silverback smashed its fists down on the car again, hitting the windscreen dead-centre. The glass fell away in clumps, covering the bonnet and the car's interior.

With the windscreen suddenly gone, Joe could see the road clearly.

He saw the brick wall coming up at seventy miles an hour.

Joe stamped on the brakes so his entire skeleton rattled as he was thrown forward in his seat. The car's tires bit the road, screeching in protest as they slid. Joe closed his eyes and clutched the steering wheel, hard enough that his knuckles went white.

The car continued its skid.

The brick wall got closer.

With a violent lurch the rubber tires finally found a grip and brought the car to a sudden stop. The whole vehicle rocked forward on its suspension. Joe's face hit the steering wheel and sent stars through his vision. He pulled himself away, dazed and bleeding. It felt as though his already-damaged nose had been pushed to the back of his skull.

The engine petered out and Joe looked out at the road. He saw the silverback lying against the brick wall several feet away, a spattering of blood and matted fur mingling with the gushing rainwater on the road. The creature was stunned, but still conscious. Joe's vision swirled as he tried to stay awake himself.

His hand shook as he reached for the key to the ignition. Shook as he turned on the engine. Shook even harder as he engaged the reverse gear.

Joe stepped down hard on the accelerator.

The car shot backward.

After twenty metres, he jammed on the brake. The tires screeched. The car stopped moving.

Into first gear and moving forward.

Second gear.

The car reached thirty.

Joe pulled into third.

"Danny, get down on the floor!"

He stamped on the brakes.

Tyres skidded on the wet road.

The car hit the wall like a missile.

Joe was out cold for several seconds. When he eventually came to, all he saw was pure white. He quickly realised that it was just the airbag deployed from the steering wheel. He pulled and pushed at it until it began to hiss and deflate. When it was finally out of the way, Joe screamed.

"It's alright, Dad," said Danny climbing forward into the passenger seat beside him. "He's dead."

Joe looked through the windscreen at the silverback's face, staring back at him from the end of the bonnet. Any spark of life had left the magnificent beast's eyes. Crushed between the wall and the vehicle, the mighty Nero, oldest inhabitant of the zoo, had died instantly. Somehow Joe found that comforting.

He turned to his son. "You okay?"

Danny nodded and smiled. "That was cool!"

Joe laughed and then threw his head back against the seat rest. "It certainly was something."

"Can we get out of here now? I haven't watched wrestling in ages."

Joe turned the key in the ignition and was astonished when the engine came back to life yet again. After such a collision it was almost a miracle that the vehicle was still willing to keep going. Joe didn't think about it too much as he reversed away from the wall and pulled out onto the main road. He was thankful for his blessings. From the chaos all around him, it seemed most others were not so lucky. Battered cars lay mangled and twisted against one another in a never-ending pile-up of ruined steel, while torn bodies littered the crimson streets like confetti. The world as they knew it was over now, the natural order forever skewed by the events of the last few days. Joe and Danny were entering a new world now, one where they were at the bottom of the food chain and wild animals roamed the lands.

But there was one thing that gave Joe hope that perhaps humanity was not quite ready to go meekly into that good night. For almost every human corpse that lay dead amongst the ruins, there was also that of a dead animal. The mutilated dogs, cats, and various other domesticated animals that littered the sidewalks told Joe one thing was for certain: people were fighting back.

There were still blessings to be found in this world, and Joe's biggest one was sitting in the seat right beside him. Joe couldn't help but smile as he and his son started their journey into the unknown, their journey into the Animal Kingdom.

EPILOGUE

RANDALL COULD HARDLY breathe amidst the cloying black smoke. It burnt at his eyes and dried out his throat. He didn't know what had started the fire, but he had a feeling that Victor had rigged some kind of explosive in case of his death.

And I witnessed that he is very much dead, indeed.

Randall placed his fingers against his temples and tried to think. He would have to leave this room soon, but then what? The animals were probably waiting for him, ready to rip him apart as soon as he stepped outside the room, and even if they were not they would most likely be waiting for him outside the building.

But I have to leave. Either that or stay and burn.

Randall stood up from the desk and hissed as he accidentally placed his broken ankle down on the floor. He pulled it back up and hopped over to the door. The smoke was hot and blinding, coming from under the door in thick, velvety waves. He closed his eyes and fumbled in his pocket for the key to the room's lock. When he found it, he wasted no time in unlocking the door.

Outside was a disorientating mixture of bright-orange flame and jet-black smoke. Randall looked left and right and saw no animals, but also saw no exit. The corridor was aflame at both ends. In front of him was the seminar room. It was no doubt where the fire had started and the books and wooden shelves would have provided all the fuel the fire needed, but now it was simply a smouldering black husk and no longer in flames.

Randall hopped through the charred doorway and instantly felt some relief from the heat of the corridor. Wind rushed in from the far side of the room and, where there had once been a wall with a window, there was now only a hole. The entire side of the building had come away. Randall hopped forward again and fell onto his hands and knees as the floor beneath him gave way.

The floor was brittle and blackened. He would have to be careful where he put his weight lest he fall right through it. He had no plan in his mind other than to remain in this room while the rest of the building burned around him. Perhaps the fire would finally attract help and bring someone to his aid.

About time the army got here.

Randall crawled forward and encountered the grizzly sight of Victor's corpse. The man's body was crisped right down to the bone and his skeleton was blackened and exposed in several places. One of the body's arms was completely missing, but Randall assumed that it was ripped off by the animals before the fire had begun.

Over at the far end of the room, Randall reached the floor end. On his chest he pushed forward until his arms and head were hanging over the edge. The air was fresher here and Randall took the opportunity to take in a series of deep breaths.

Beneath him the animals went wild as they spotted him. Hooting, barking, screeching and making an all manner of inhuman noises, they glared up at him with hunger in their eyes.

Whilst the animal army had thinned, it was still approaching a hundred in its number, mostly smaller creatures, now, like warthogs and llamas. They surrounded the building and never once took their eyes off Randall.

Randall pushed himself back up onto his knees and then slowly up onto his one good leg. He looked down at the animals and spat. The globule of spit was lost in the billowing smoke and he did not know if it hit a target. He bellowed with laughter.

"You will not have me! A leader chooses his own death." Randall placed a hand over his heart as if he were addressing the nation from some great palatial balcony. "And as any great leader would do, I choose to go down with my ship."

Randall stretched his arms out wide on either side of him and looked up and the grey sky. At that exact moment the gentle drizzle burst into a full-grown downpour. Randall took it as a sign. "Deliver me, Lord, from my enemies. They shall not have me." He looked down at the baying animals below. "You hear that, you fuckers? You shall not have me."

Randall leapt, expecting to feel the wind through his hair as he plummeted towards salvation, towards the next life.

All he felt was the floor as his entire body splintered upon impact. Not a single muscle in his entire body would answer him as he lay there, still – but he was not dead. He knew that much. As he lay there, he saw an ant scuttle towards him and into his ear. The feeling was intense and vivid. Somehow the fall had not dulled his senses. As the animals surrounded his body, he knew that it was going to be the worst and final agony of his life. They began to eat him alive.

The pain was a hundred times worse than anything he ever imagined.

And it went on forever.

ABOUT THE AUTHOR

Iain Rob Wright is from the English town of Redditch, where he worked for many years as a mobile telephone salesman. After publishing his debut novel, THE FINAL WINTER, in 2011 to great success, he quit his job and became a full time writer. He now has over a dozen novels, and in 2013 he co-wrote a book with bestselling author, J.A.Konrath.

WWW.IAINROBWRIGHT.COM

43553556R00130

Made in the USA
Middletown, DE
25 April 2019